Heidi

# The Witch Of Weasel Warren

Have a spooky adventure!

Oct 14, 2023

# The Witch Of Weasel Warren

A Story by
Bruce Kilby

Illustrated by
Dallas Lenton

This is a work of fiction. Names, characters, places and incidences are the products of the authors' imagination or are used fictitiously. Any resemblance to actual events, locales, or people, living or dead, is entirely coincidental.

Published by Fireside Stories Publishing

#8 5662 208th Street,
Langley, B.C., Canada
V3A 8G1

Editing, Interior Design, and Cover Design:
Wendy Dewar Hughes, Summer Bay Press



E-book readers can obtain the accompanying music CD music, and chapter plates for youngsters to colour can be downloaded from the website at Firesidestoriespublishing.com.

Print ISBN: 978-0-9920742-2-7

Digital ISBN: 978-0-9920742-1-0

# Dedication

To my wife, Michelle

My inspiring hero who faced incredible life challenges

with unbelievable courage.

The concept of the Witch of Weasel Warren was based on songs written and produced by Don Thompson of Studio 56. As a long time friend, he allowed me to use the title as inspiration for the book and I thank him from the bottom of my heart. I have included those songs with the book to give him the credit he so richly deserves.

I want to thank Dallas Lenton who breathed life into each of the book's characters with his phenomenal artistic skills. Amid a hectic life he devoted himself to his work creating timeless classics for generations to enjoy. I truly believe Dallas will be a bright star in the world of illustrators.

Finally, I thank the ever-valiant Wendy Dewar Hughes of Summer Bay Press who carefully and skillfully edited each page all the while dealing with the often grammatically flawed storyteller. She is also responsible for the book's design.

I thank you all.

## Contents


| | | |
|---|---|---|
| Prologue | | 2 |
| Chapter 1 | Something Strange Going On | 10 |
| Chapter 2 | Morning Warning | 20 |
| Chapter 3 | Listen to ME! | 32 |
| Chapter 4 | Quacks the Pig | 40 |
| Chapter 5 | The Witch and Weasels | 54 |
| Chapter 6 | The Night Watch | 62 |
| Chapter 7 | Potion in Motion | 78 |
| Chapter 8 | What to Do | 94 |
| Chapter 9 | The Petting Zoo | 110 |
| Chapter 10 | Gerome the Gnome | 126 |
| Chapter 11 | Oberon's Amulet | 140 |
| Chapter 12 | Northwoods Roost | 154 |
| Chapter 13 | Sugarplum Returns | 164 |
| Chapter 14 | The Day of Haunting | 180 |
| Chapter 15 | The Hour of the witch | 190 |
| Chapter 16 | Something More Evil Going On | 200 |
| Chapter17 | Good vs. Evil | 212 |
| Chapter 18 | Back on the Farm | 240 |

# Prologue

Before the age of darkness, and before the weeds of evil wrapped around men's hearts, the world was a garden of peace. Harmony and balance allowed all that dwelled within it to live without fear, without want, and in graceful tranquility.

Griffins, centaurs, unicorns and winged Pegasus roamed the earth uninhibited and unaware of dark hearts harboring wickedness. Fairies, elves and gnomes were free to help Mother Nature create all her wonders and man, charged with tending the earth, never hungered or thirst. The soil, rivers, lakes, and oceans gave him all he could ever need. The world was as it was meant to be.

Unfortunately, over time, man got tired of passing days lavished in honey, sunshine, frolic, and idle play. No matter how much joy one could possess, an evil seed of desire started to grow in the dark corners of their hearts. Slowly at first, this disease crept insidiously in, wrapping tightly around his goodwill and bliss. He became increasingly moody and unsatisfied, distrustful and suspicious; his moods grew darker and foreboding and anger seethed inside of him. He wanted more and when man wants more, he will do or promise anything—anything at all to get it.

Like poisonous venom seeping through his veins, jealousy, greed, and the need for power gradually took over his patient and compassionate being. No matter what Mother Nature provided him it was now never enough. Some say this was all planned by evil forces hidden deep in the underworld, or perhaps it had always been there veiled in man's character but whatever it was, there were plenty of beings in the dark world willing to give man anything his heart desired, for a price, of course.

These dark creatures with evil in their souls were tired of being trapped in caverns deep in the earth or the infernos of the nether world. They yearned for their freedom to roam the upper world and in doing so, dominate and control it. Unbeknownst to man, these creatures wanted most of all to crush and defeat the human soul, take the essence of people's lives and turn them into minions of evil to do with as they willed.

For some humans, these temptations were too strong and they succumbed to the glitter of this evil magic. At first, all seemed amusing as the fallen few relished their new wealth and power. Their treasure chests overflowed with gold, diamonds, rubies, and pearls but still, niggling at their souls, the lust for power and greed kept growing and, as is the human tendency, they were never satisfied.

As these desires and black hearts flourished, they turned their sly eyes toward whatever anyone else possessed. Enslaved by thirst for power, acts of betrayal and distrust, the ever-increasing resentment of others soon led to threats and disputes. They declared themselves chieftains, kings, emperors and sovereigns and endowed themselves with divine rights having undeniable power. More and better-crafted weapons, and higher and thicker walls were created to protect what they deemed theirs and to intimidate others who keenly wanted what they possessed. It did not take long before ferocious wars broke out between tribes, fiefdoms then the kingdoms themselves.

No matter how much the good and peaceful forces tried to fight off the approaching evil, the world darkened and lay in despair for many, many years.

All magic, as you might expect, starts to fade over time. Those with power had to make increasingly more to exalt in the same exhilaration of power. But as with all things too good to be true, there was a price to pay. With continued use of additional supernatural enchantments, more and more of their humanity left them. Slowly, their minds, bodies, and souls started to change into something they were never intended to be.

Before long, these demons gained their unfettered freedom. Banshees, golems, gargoyles and dragons roamed the earth wreaking carnage to all who dared to cross their paths. Humans changed into half-men, half-beasts, gorgons and mermaids. This was not what these humans had bargained for but the lust for power had relentlessly tugged at them with unseen dark spirits until they could refuse no longer. They were eternally trapped into the spiral of doom and the tight clutches of evil.

There were those, of course, who wanted a different kind of power. They did not want riches, land, or sit on thrones; they wanted a darker ethereal power to control both man and beast. Black witches and warlocks performed rituals, brewed potions, and cast spells all in the quest for more and stronger black magic. White magic and natural powers were just not enough to satisfy these diminished souls and, though warned by Mother Nature, temptation overpowered them into thinking they could reign in the sinister power of the underworld. They delved deeper and deeper into the craft of black magic, taking the good magic of the elves, fairies, and gnomes and changing it into something more sinister, more evil.

Under the weight of all this wickedness, their faces grew grotesque and pale, their shoulders slumped and backs hunched. They became something very different from what we would call human. Once changed, to enter the world of humans they needed to disguise themselves so as to appear as normal mortals and hide their true selves. To remain on the surface world without being discovered, they were forced to conjure magic potions and spells to mask their true character and, as with other enchantments, they needed to use more and more of their sinister black magic. The more they used, the more they changed and the more they changed, the more grotesque they became.

Eventually, the whole earth became embroiled in the war between good and bad, demon and holy, and of course, white and black magic. For centuries this internal war raged on. Fairies, elves, gnomes, and the humans unwilling to bend toward the darkness, fought desperately to return the earth to its natural balance. Evil, on the other hand, fought feverishly to keep the world in darkness and torment.

To protect their homeland from discovery by hunters, and with their growing distrust of humans who at any time could turn to the dark side, the fairies hid their Fairylands from most of the world's creatures. These magical places were hidden behind secret walls and doors in the forests, mountains, and faraway places. Only a fairy, gnome, or elf could reveal the entrances to these magical places.

It is said that, unlike elves and gnomes, a fairy with her wand could conjure a door anywhere he or she pleased purely by a sprinkle of stardust. All other creatures had to know the locations of the secret pathways and hidden doorways in order to enter Fairyland. Many mythical beasts, like unicorns and Pegasus', were embraced in these realms as they were mercilessly hunted and prized by many, especially the forces of evil, for their astonishing magical qualities.

After many desperate years, countless ogres and other mystical beasts were driven back into the murky depths of darkness. Dragons were fought, evil minions conquered, and spells broken by the elfin guardians and their human friends, but not all evil creatures returned from whence they had come. Eventually, the forces of good gained the upper hand but never truly won the battle.

Today, the conflict still rages. Unseen by most, always in the shadowy background, the sentinels of good attempt to protect the innocent by keeping vigil on those that may remain and an ever watchful eye for the slightest sign of sinister dark forces attempting to return.

A few of these ominous beings, undiscovered by the sentinels, stay out of sight in the human world to create nightmares and legends and to forever tempt weak men. Biding their time, these creatures willingly lie unobserved, waiting until they can release the ever-ready and ever-present armies of darkness to once again prey upon the world—our world.

Those humans who have succumbed to evil whom we call witches and warlocks, continue to scheme for their dark masters to return. They eternally look for gateways to the underworld in hopes of releasing these fiends onto a now unsuspecting and innocent world. They dream of having ultimate power over humanity once again.

As a reminder to all of what will happen to those who choose evil, Oberon, King of the Fairies, had an amulet made by the gnomes for his wife, Queen Titania. The magic amulet held a supernatural gem that would turn into sinister monuments of stone all gargoyles, dragons, and other such evil creatures that refused to return to their underworld. He thought that this would serves as a deterrent to all who wished to possess wickedness, as these creatures would be forever on display as motionless statues of granite.

Humans have since carved replicas of these creatures on the walls of castles, temples, totem poles, and gateways to remind future generations of the pending evil forces but over time, humans have long since forgotten the battles; they have forgotten the warnings of their ancestors and what should happen to reward the choice of evil. They think of them only as legends to scare children. They pass them off as mere…fairytales.

However, the creatures of evil have never forgotten their pain and are still forever lurking in the darkness, waiting and wanting revenge.

Many years later, while on a trip to the human world, Queen Titania, disguised in human form, had come to assist several gnomes to return a particularly resistant ghost back into his grave. Suddenly, one, then two, then three skeletal hands thrust up from their resting place, through the soil, and clutched at her. They clawed at her ankles, grasped her knees then gripped her arms and began tugging her into an open grave. It happened so quickly that she had no time to cast her Shatter Spell or transform back into fairy form. Abruptly, a dark-cloaked figure sprang from a shadow and snatched the amulet from the chain around her neck then just as quickly disappeared in a puff of foul, grey smoke.

Bruce Kilby

# Chapter 1

## Something Strange Going On

The silver shimmer from a full, late October moon glistened off the oily black feathers of Duke Skysquawker, as he made his usual midnight flight over the tiny village of Weasel Warren. Weasel Warren lay just outside the little town of Badgerville, which indeed, was in the middle of nowhere.

All the forest animals called the crows that roosted in the Northwoods, Skysquawkers due to their incessant noise, especially around nesting time, and at dawn, sunset, or any time they objected to anything or anyone coming near the roost. It seemed to the other animals, wild or domestic, that the crows objected to nearly everything.

Duke could feel the early frost in the cool, crisp air and hear the whisper of the wind rush over his outstretched wings as he began his nightly forage for food. After the sun went down, his eyes, like hard, black beads, darted to and fro, searching for tasty morsels left behind by other scavengers or careless humans.

He was not picky; anything would do to satisfy the burning hunger in the bottom of his belly. Scraps left over from a tipped-over garbage can, ransacked by raccoons perhaps, or a discarded chicken bone, or an apple or two out of reach of the pickers—anything would suit. His sharp black beak could flip open a cardboard pizza box and snatch a scrap of leftover crust from the dumpster behind Mario's Pizza before the alley cats even knew he was there!

"Caw, I don't understand humans. I don't understand humans at all! Caw, waste, waste, waste! Why would they throw tasty food away? Let their food rot in that tin bin? Tin bin! Food, food, delicious food. Caw."

Duke Skysquawker preferred to scavenge in the night shadows when there was less competition. He didn't have to worry about his noisy fellow crows, prowling house cats, or sniffing dogs. He could feast at his leisure and didn't have to share! Mind you, he did have to fight off the odd rat, raccoon, or alley cat but he was tougher and more daring than the other skittish night prowlers. Once Duke had his eyes on a morsel, almost nothing could scare him away.

The colour of the blackest night, Duke was also invisible to any other predator wishing to make him its supper. "Caw, caw, fool them, I can, hide, I can, caw, caw,"

The only ones who truly gave him trouble were those pesky humans, always shooing him away or blasting at him with those fire sticks. There was also that strange straw man who stood still in the field with his arms outstretched all day long, his ragged coat flapping in the breeze. He made Duke nervous.

"Caw. Scare me he do, scare me. Caw!"

The twisting, turning stone paths that ran through the forest west of Weasel Warren held one of Duke's favourite feeding haunts. Many an unfortunate forest animal met an untimely end while crossing these paths, murdered by the foul-smelling, ruthless metal beasts that roared past and screeched on the surface of the road. Lifeless when stopped, these creatures could spring to life and roar away without notice, so even though Duke had ventured as far as to land on one's top, he remained leery of getting too close.

It did not escape his notice however, that these machines were expert hunters. They would trap his furry friends in the glare of two bright eyes glowing out into the night and race toward them! His friends froze where they stood hoping not to be seen, just as they would in the forest.

"Caw, a big mistake, big mistake!" Duke cackled to himself. "Got to be watchful, yes, very careful."

What was even more confusing was that these great beasts never ate their kill. They seemed to hunt, charge, and strike down their prey, then dead or alive, leave it on the road!

"Caw, more for me, me, me, me. Caw!" he shrieked with delight. "Fly if they can; run if they can't! Caw! Caw!"

He did not know what hold humans had over these metal beasts. He had seen them permit humans into their tummies then allow them to come and go as they pleased—without eating them! Duke could not understand it at all.

"Caw, humans must taste bad! Bad, bad, bad," he reasoned.

As with all crows, Duke had a very keen eye and an uncanny sense when it came to finding road kill or scraps of garbage tossed carelessly away by humans. Tonight, Duke was in a jolly mood. He could almost guarantee a meal beyond compare on Fridays.

"Caw, a beautiful feast, indeed! Hmm…very tasty, yes. Tasty, tasty, tasty!"

Duke had come to realize that this was the night for human juveniles to get together on something they called "dates." For Duke, this was a rich opportunity for glorious food. They always brought yummy food.

These nights always ended with the young humans inside the metal beasts pressing their faces together, overlooking Weasel Warren from the top of Rapture Ridge.

"Caw, why do they do that? Silly, silly, silly! Peck, peck, peck. Caw."

All he knew was that they would wrap their wings around each other and press their beaks together. The metal beasts' glassy eyes would then grow foggy.

"Caw, caw, can't take your eye off your food! No, siree, not with me around! Keep an eye on the food. Food, food, food!"

Duke knew that before the human young went to the ridge, they would stop at Sonny Joe's Hamburger stand, get brown bags full of wonderful-smelling, beak-licking goodies. He could never understand why they would then roar through the winding stone paths of the forest trying to kill his friends. A flock of them would race up and finally stop the metal beast on Rapture Ridge. He could smell those irresistible aromas oozing from the bellies of the beasts.

He could already taste the half-eaten flat pieces of meat in round bread tossed from the dimly lit cavities of the metal beasts. Why would humans throw food away? It was against the animal kingdom code. For Duke, though, it meant no hunting his own. "So tempting, tempting, tempting, tempting," he chortled, ruffling his feathers. In the beginning, he thought it was a trap but over time he learned that humans were just...wasteful.

"Caw, Caw, going to eat well tonight, yup, eat good, good, good," he squawked.

Duke had perfected the trick of landing on the big, warm nose of the beast and pretending his leg had broken. He hobbled across the warm hood looking pathetic. That's when the female humans would often feel sorry for him and throw a tasty morsel from the window as he eagerly snatched up the pieces. "No onion rings. Don't like onions," he cackled.

No salt, not good, not good for Duke he thought. Vinegar, bad vinegar, tastes bad, taste bad, bad!

Sometimes the teens played jokes on him by tossing a hot pepper out then they'd giggle as he shook his head cool the scorching taste, opening his beak to chill his throat.

"Caw, Caw, hot, hot!" How can humans eat that stuff? "Too hot, hot, hot!"

The male humans offered pieces of bread or potato stick from their hands, enticing him closer. "Caw, tempting yes, very, very tempting, not going to get trapped. Not too close. Not going to get me, not going to get me!"

Patience then a quick snatch and he was away. He flew up to his favorite perch in a Nobel pine to watch, waiting for the right moment. "Caw, maybe I can steal the whole bag when they are too busy pressing faces!"

But tonight would be different from Duke's usual Friday night activities. On his weekly flight to Rapture Mountain and the delectable late night supper that waited there, Duke caught in the corner of his eye something very unusual at McSimmons' farm—something very unusual indeed.

Shadowy movements in the southeast corner of Farmer McSimmons' famous pumpkin patch caught his eye. Inquisitive as always, he tilted his wing and soared in a graceful circle for a better look.

McSimmons grew the biggest, fattest pumpkins in the county. For the past three years, he had won the Weasel Warren Pumpkin Harvest Festival with pumpkins so big only one could fit in the back of his groaning truck. This year would be no different. Duke loved nothing better than to feast on those left behind, orange balls rotting in the field as winter came but tonight, he saw something very odd going on.

"Caw, Caw. Hello, hello, what's going on here then?" he called as he looked down over the patch. "There's something not right here, not right. Right, right, right," he squawked. Turning his head from one side to the other to get a better look, Duke couldn't believe his eyes. The pumpkins appeared to move and slide across the frosty ground all by themselves!

"Caw, Caw, strange, strange, strange!" he said, blinking twice. The scarecrow stood motionless in the middle of the field. Duke coasted in a little closer.

The orange globes formed into a single line, moving out of the pumpkin patch and into the nearby woods. Circling stealthily down, Duke saw several dark shapes scurrying around, supporting each orange orb. Carrying, pushing, and pulling, these cloaked creatures systematically stripping the field of its pumpkins.

"Caw, who would want to take pumpkins? Farmer McSimmons' pumpkins Who? who? who?!" he cawed.

As he made one more low pass above the shadowy figures, he recognized a telltale sign peeking out from under a midnight marauder's hooded cloak. It was the long, bushy tail of one of the most cunning, skulking, conniving, and bad-tempered of all forest rodents.

"CAW, WEASELS! CAW, WEASELS!" he shrieked in alarm, frantically flapping his wings. "Weasels, weasels, weasels!"

Now, crows have hated weasels since the beginning of time. These thieves crept up the tall trees in the springtime to find the crows' nests when left unattended, and loved to make meals of their precious baby eggs.

"Caw, those varmints! Varmints, varmints, varmints. Those low down sneaky varmints!" he squawked. "What would they want with pumpkins, pumpkins, pumpkins?" He could see them chewing through the stems and pushing the pumpkins toward the fence. "Caw, Caw they're up to no good, up to no good. I just know it! Weasels! Caw, caw, caw!"

With Duke's noise overhead, weasels realized that their night raid had been exposed.

"Crow! Crow!" the leader yelled. "Scram, everybody!"

"Let's get outta here!" another hissed.

In a blink of a crow's eye, they dropped their booty, scurried to the old wooden fence, squeezed under it and disappeared into the ebony shadows of the Northwoods. Within a heartbeat it seemed like they had never been there at all.

Duke realized that he had not heard one hoot, chirp, or even a bullfrog's croak on his flight to Rapture Ridge. The night had taken on an eerie silence that only a pack of weasels could generate.

"Caw, should have known, should have known, known, known! Weasels near, weasels near," he admonished himself as he landed on a fence post.

The moon slid behind a dark cloud, hiding the muddy field and the last of the escaping weasels. Seeing nothing more, he took off again. "Won't be a next time, no sir, no next time for sure, for sure." His raucous caw rang through the midnight darkness, as the familiar wind raced over his outstretched wings.

"Caw, Caw. Got to tell someone! Someone has to know! For sure, for sure. They gotta know," his hoarse voice announced. "Got to tell someone, got to tell! Tell, tell, tell," he squawked as he took off toward the McSimmons farm.

Because of his midnight detour, Duke would go hungry tonight. The rats, raccoons, coyotes, and other night prowlers would have stripped the ridge of every delicious scrap of roadside feast. There would not be so much as a crust of leftover pizza or a cold potato stick left for him.

As he flew away, no one noticed the lonely scarecrow, standing in the middle of the pumpkin field, take on a strange blue glow and shudder as if trying to unearth itself from its stationery place.

Bruce Kilby

# Chapter 2

# Morning Warning

Duke flung himself through the night sky toward McSimmons' farmhouse. He had to raise the alarm somehow.

"Sneezer! Caw, Sneezer! Sneezer, Sneezer!" he wheezed as his scaly feet curled around the telephone line. At his current speed, his whole body whipped twice around the wire before ending upright.

Duke knew that if one friend could help, it was the farm's faithful watchdog, Sneezer. Even though Sneezer was a bloodhound, he was no longer much good at hunting. At one time, he could smell a raccoon a hundred yards away if the wind was just right. He would poke his nose up in the air and sniff the scent, eyes narrowed. Now though, his job was simply to woof if strangers came around, protect the farm animals from prey such as foxes, coyotes, and wolves, and of course, protect the crops from crows. He protected the apples trees, cherries trees, and the wheat in the fields—from crows.

"Caw, Sneezer! Caw, Sneezer!" Duke squawked as he leapt off the wire and flapped downward, landing on the peak of Sneezer's doghouse. "Caw, Caw, Caw!" he called, trying to wake the snoozing hound.

Unaware of the commotion, Sneezer, dutifully nestled in his black dog sweater with the word SECURITY hand-sewn on the back, was lost in one of his favorite dreams. Tonight, as with most nights, he relived his youth by giving chase to a skedaddling rabbit in his dreams. He lay half out of his dog house snorting and whining, long floppy ears twitching and paws jerking as if he were once again tracking a hare through the fields.

"Caw, Caw, Caw! Security alert, security alert!" Duke repeated, flapping his wings in frustration.

"I'm gonna get ya, I'm gonna..." Sneezer mumbled in his sleep. His white whiskers glowed in the pale moonlight.

"Hopeless, hopeless," Duke cawed. "Caw, Caw." He had to do something.

He cast about with his black eyes and noticed Sneezer's chewing bone propped between his paws. "Caw, caw. If I hit it just right, just right..." He jumped off the roof and landed heavily on the end of the bone.

"Yeow!" Sneezer howled. The bone pinched his paws then flipped and hurtled upward. Startled, Sneezer leapt up, hitting his head on the doorway of the doghouse. "Yeow-ow!"

They both watched the bone reach its apex and then start to tumble down. Splash! It landed his water dish, flipping it into the air. Both the dish and its contents landed smack on Sneezer's head.

Soaked but very much awake now, Sneeze whined, "Wha, Wha, What did you do that for?"

"Some security, some security you are! Caw, caw." Duke's head bobbed as he jumped up and down, wings a-flutter. "I could have been a burglar, or a murderer! Caw, caw."

"I was awake. I was awake, yesiree. Sharp as a tack. That's me!"

"Caw, liar, liar, tail on fire. Tail on fire."

"What...?" Duke said turning to look at his tail. "It's not on fire... Oh, you're just fooling me."

"Caw, sharp as a tack, my boy. Sharp as a tack."

"Now what do you want?" Sneezer asked, drawing himself up before flopping back down on his belly.

"Caw, Caw, Caw! There's something going on, something going on down at the pumpkin patch! Caw, caw, caw!"

"Shhhhhhh, Shhhhhh, you'll wake Farmer McSimmons!" Sneezer whispered, pressing a big paw onto Duke's bobbing head. Sneezer cast a nervous eye up to the bedroom window but no lights came on in the farmhouse.

"You don't ever want him coming down at night 'cause he'll start blasting!" he muttered hoarsely. "Ya don't want that, do ya?"

Duke sighed and peered out from under Sneezer's great paw. They both knew that it was not usual for a crow to be friends with a dog. A few years before, Sneezer developed allergies to almost everything. He couldn't smell a pea without sneezing ten times. Tracking was out of the question. He always ended up in a sneezing fit, alerting game and allowing them to escape unharmed. One day Molly, the horse, unofficially changed the dog's name from Snickers to Sneezer. The name stuck.

Farmer McSimmons, who liked to hunt pheasant, grouse, or goose for family dinners, could no longer hunt with the sneezing hound. Hunting predators like foxes, wolves, and coyotes was also out of the question.

"Well, Snick," Farmer McSimmons said one day, "you're not much good to me now, old boy. We can't keep feedin' a dog that can't pull his weight. I guess..." he wiped a tear from his eye with his well used handkerchief, "I'm just gonna have to put you down."

Farm animals know this spells disaster. Losing an old friend would upset the whole farm. The older animals had seen times when Farmer McSimmons had to put down sick friends, not because he wanted to but because he did not want them to suffer pain. But Snickers wasn't sick or unable to get around, he was just…old.

When the animals around the farm heard McSimmons' proclamation not one wanted Sneezer killed before his natural time. They knew they had to do something. They couldn't hide him; he would be found. He would never last in the wild. The farm council called a meeting.

The farm council was led by Quacks the Pig, the patriarch of the farm. The orphaned pig had been raised by Mildred the Mallard who was too old have any more ducklings. She had protested profusely when she had been elected by the farm council to raise the little piglet.

"Quack, quack, quack, quack, how am I to do that? I don't know how to raise a pig!" she objected, prancing around in a circle. "He can't swim; he has no webbed feet! He can't fly; he has no feathers or even wings. He can't even pretend to fly!" She grew more and more excited. "He has no beak, so how can I teach him to preen himself and keep clean?' She received little sympathy from the council.

"There are no experienced mothers available," they claimed, apologizing. "No sows, ewes, or mares. We know you can do it."

"He's little now but do you know how big these things grow? He'll eat me out of nest and home! Think of the mess he'll make! I'll be the laughing stock of the flock! I don't mind an ugly duckling but a pig? I can't do this, quack, I can't do this... take him back."

Her protests fell on deaf ears. She was the only mother available and she had been elected by the farm council to raise the pig. And that was the end of that.

When Quacks was small, Duke and the other crows roosted in the nearby trees squawking with delight at the sight of a pig splashing about in the duck pond during swimming lessons. They thought it was a funny sight indeed. The other ducklings paddled gracefully around the pond while Quacks almost drowned daily as he floundered, swallowing more water than air. Mildred pecked at his legs until he got the hang of his awkward piggy paddle.

Quacks soon grew into a fine fellow and a good swimmer and because he could speak both beast and foul, he became the farm patriarch.

When the time had come for Sneezer to be put down, the farm council, even after much debate, could still not come up with a solution. It was Quacks alone who hatched the plan. Cocking one eyebrow up, he declared, "My friends, I'll call it, Morning Warning!"

A murmur of surprise rippled through the council.

On the eve of Sneezer's intended demise, Quacks had overheard Farmer McSimmons, and called the crows in from the Northwoods rookery to attend the emergency council meeting. The crows were reluctant to attend, as there had always been an unwritten rule that wild stayed wild and domestic stayed domestic. It was nature's way. The very term "murder of crows" struck fear in the hearts of tamed animals.

The crows preferred it be called a "rookery" even though they weren't rooks. The name sounded less menacing. The animal kingdom knew the birds were simply scavengers, not murderers but lore and reputation were hard to dispel. The farm elders were nervous.

Quacks called for silence. The crows, perched on every rafter, rail, and crossbeam in the old barn, chattered and squabbled so loudly Quacks that had to ring Daisy's cow bell several times to quiet them down.

"Okay, listen up here. Hush, everyone! I need some quiet now. We need to get on with the meeting before Mr. and Mrs. McSimmons wake up." A sudden hush fell over the barn. Every one of them knew about Farmer McSimmons' thunder stick.

"Now that I have your attention, I don't need to remind you that we have a serious situation facing us." His voice became solemn. "As you know, our dear old friend Sneezer is set to be put down tomorrow morning unless we come up with a plan to save him."

"Ya mean dead?" asked Barley, the donkey.

"Yup! Pushing up daisies dead," Quacks replied.

"Oooooh," the crowd gasped in unison.

"Quack, quack. Why are the crows here?" gabbled Mildred. "You know they steal everything! Don't turn your back on those black soulless demons!" She took a quavering breath. "Do you know how many eggs they have stolen from my nests?"

"I don't trust them, not for an inch!" cried Henrietta the chicken. "They are always after my chicks and breaking my eggs. I don't trust them one bit!"

The geese ran in circles, flustered at even the presence of the untrustworthy scavengers within their midst.

"Quiet, quiet, please!' Quacks pleaded. "I know our neighbours have not always been, shall we say, polite, but please hear out my plan. We might just have a way to save Sneezer and for all of us to live together in harmony." He drew out the final word.

A great din of dispute swelled from the frenzied crowd. Protesting or agreeing, it did not matter. Nobody could understand a word anyone else said anyway.

"What was that?" Henrietta said.

"Huh?" said Penny the Pig.

"Who said that?" asked Barley.

"I'm ready for war!" said Angus the bull, stomping his hoof and snorting. "Who wants WAR?"

"Quiet please, please. There'll be no war today," Quacks interrupted, raising his voice to a squeal. "Please just listen and all will become clear."

The din quieted down to a muffled rumble. Quacks cleared his throat. "I know there is much distrust between those of us on the farm and our Northwood neighbours and undomesticated others."

Another murmur of agreement rippled through the crowd.

"I also know that you crows have taken many losses at the hands of Farmer McSimmons and his thunder stick each time he found you in his cherry trees, apple trees, and the wheat and pumpkin fields!"

"Caw, Caw, Caw!" came the reply with lots of black heads bobbing.

Barley, the donkey, turned to Molly. "What did he say?"

"I don't understand Crow," she told him.

"Crow, what about crow?" Barley asked.

"Eat crow, you old coot! You're deaf!" Molly shouted into the donkey's ear.

"Listen everybody," Quacks continued. "We have one chance to mend our nests." He glanced around the room to ensure he had everyone's attention. "We have to prove to Farmer McSimmons that Sneezer is worth keeping." A murmur of agreement swirled through the crowd. "And the crows need a safe way to hunt for food."

A cry of dismay rose from the farm animals.

"Listen, if we can resolve this, your chicks, your eggs, Mildred and Henrietta, your corn, Barley, Molly, and Daisy, would all be safe."

"How do we do that?" Barley asked.

"We let them have it!" Quacks replied.

"What?" They all gasped in disbelief.

"Humph. I'll let them have it!" snorted Angus. "Let me at them. I'll let them have it, right between the eyes!"

"Are you sure?" asked Molly.

"If we let the crows eat the cherries or feast in the fields, they will leave our eggs, our chicks, and our feed alone."

"But McSimmons will shoot them!" Henrietta wailed. "I don't like violence on the farm."

"Okay by me!" Angus said. "Wait a minute, Let me think about it..." he paused. "Nope, I'm over it! Okay by me!"

"No, no, no!" said Quacks raising his hoof to quiet them down again.

"Caw, we agree, we agree!" said the crows most eagerly.

"Of course, they would agree," squawked Henrietta.

"Look, we can lose a few cherries and apples at the top of the trees. The pickers can't reach them anyway. The fields have so many pumpkins, wheat, and barley the McSimmons' won't miss the few pounds these guys eat. So what do you say?" Quacks looked at the faces in the crowd and saw heads nodding.

"If they promise to leave the eggs and chicks alone," said Mildred.

"And our feed," said Molly and Bailey together.

"Caw, caw, caw, yes, yes, yes!" said the crows thinking of delicious banquets and filling their stomachs without fear.

"Hush, you darn Skysquawkers," quacked Mildred.

Quacks continued again. "When the crows come, like they always do, in the early morning to feast on the fields and trees, Sneezer…hey, Sneezer, are you listening?" Quacks nudged Sneezer awake.

"Huh, oh yes, I'm awake, I'm awake...who goes there?" he yipped.

"Sneezer will start to howl when he sees McSimmons coming out with the thunder stick and charge off after the crows. Being warned, the crows will fly away to safety."

"Yup, that's me, runnin' after the crows."

"What does that prove?" asked Barley.

"Don't you get it? Farmer McSimmons will think Sneezer is doing his job by alerting him of the crows in the trees and chasing them away! I call it the Morning Warning! All Sneezer has to do is run ahead of McSimmons howling his head off. McSimmons will think Sneezer is chasing the birds away to save his crop. He'll really be warning the crows to get away!"

"Ahhhh," the crowd said, nodding. The crows bobbed up and down in excitement.

"Can I have a vote from Council then?"

"AYE!" echoed through the barn.

"Any against?"

"I don't get it," said Barley.

"Carried!" Quacks said, ringing Molly's bell. "Then it is settled."

The next morning just as the sun pushed its first golden rays over the horizon, the rooster crowed his daily wakeup bugle call and as planned, the crows were filling their bellies with cherries in Farmer McSimmons' orchard. Squawking with such a racket, the crows could hardly believe their fortune of getting to enjoy such a feast without danger.

Farmer McSimmons, as if on cue, rushed out of the farmhouse with his overalls half slung over one shoulder and a shotgun in one hand, jamming his hat on his head with the other.

"What in tarnation is going on 'round here?" he hollered cocking his shotgun. "Those darn crows! Let me at 'em!"

As arranged, Sneezer had dutifully dashed off toward the orchard howling at the birds. On cue the crows fled the scene in one black flock. By the time Farmer McSimmons fired several shots at them, the crows were too far away for the buckshot to find any targets. Duke trotted back, wagging his tail, head held high.

"Good boy, Snick!" was all that was said. It was all that was necessary. The farmer smiled at his dog and gave him a loving scratch behind the ear.

Sneezer might no longer be a bloodhound who was any good at hunting but he was still the official farm guard dog. The crisis was over. The plan had worked. Mrs. McSimmons knitted a black sweater for Sneezer to wear with the word SECURITY in white letters sewed in on the back.

Ever since that day, the crows, Duke, and Sneezer became trusted friends and over time they even came to understand each other's languages.

Bruce Kilby

# Chapter 3

## Listen to ME!

Inside the cozy old farmhouse and up the narrow stairs, Mr. and Mrs. McSimmons lay sound asleep in their overstuffed feather bed. Mr. McSimmons loved to wear his horse print pajamas while Mrs. McSimmons wore a ruffled-neck, full-length, cotton nightgown. Her hair was in curlers and she had the covers tugged right up to her chin. Farmer McSimmons' leg stuck out of the covers on his side of the bed as he had only one-foot width of bed to sleep on. Mrs. McSimmons sprawled across the rest of the mattress.

Mr. McSimmons' snoring broke rhythm for only a second with Duke's racket. He mumbled, "Wha...what was that noise?" then resumed his inhaled rumble and exhaled whistle.

The cotton wool in Mrs. McSimmons ears ensured she would not hear Duke, Mr. McSimmons, or anything else until the rooster crowed at five.

"Hmph, Caw, Caw! Breathe, I can't breathe!" Duke finally gasped, springing free of Sneezer's paw. "Caw!" he rasped, out of breath. "I said, there's something going on down at the pumpkin patch! Down at the pumpkin patch! I saw it. I saw it!"

"Okay, okay, I heard you. What did you see, little friend?" Sneezer muttered.

"Caw, the pumpkins, the pumpkins, caw."

"Okay, pumpkins are meant to be in the pumpkin patch! At least I thought so," Sneezer replied. "Did you say hello to Patches the Scarecrow while you were there?" He squinted at the bird.

"Caw, no, no time, he's a stick in the mud, stick in the mud, he never says anything to me, boring, boring, bor- ring! Just twirls his scary whirly birds!" he stammered. "Scary, scary. Caw."

"Oh, he really is a nice fellow once you get to know him."

"Never mind the scarecrow! The pumpkins were moving! The pumpkins were moving out of the pumpkin patch. All in a row; moving!" He hopped about, flapping his wings.

"Hmmm. That is very strange. Why do you think they would do that? I've never seen pumpkins move before. They just sit there and get fat!"

"Caw, the weasels, the weasels!"

"I thought you were talking about pumpkins? Weasels aren't fat. They're sneaky and, and...weasely."

"Caw, caw," Duke cried, cuffing Sneezer's ear with a black wing. "The weasels were stealing the pumpkins! Stealing the pumpkins!"

"Why would weasels want to steal the pumpkins this close to Halloween?" Sneezer asked, scratching his clobbered ear with a hind paw.

Now Duke knew that Sneezer had never been the smartest of canines. "Caw, don't know, don't know. That's why I came here, tell someone, tell someone."

"The children will be kind of disappointed if they can't carve a pumpkin for Halloween. And Mrs McSimmons loves to make her famous pumpkin pies!" Sneezer drawled, sniffing the air as if to relish the delectable scent of fresh-baked pie. "Aaaachoooo! Aaaachoooo!

Aaaachoooo! Aaaachoooo!" he sneezed. When finally able to come up for air he wheezed, "That was a mistake." He dropped his runny nose onto his front paws again.

"Caw, Caw," Duke said, slapping his forehead in disbelief. "Are you that? No never mind, never mind," he muttered. "That's why I came to see YOU!"

"Me? Why me? I don't know anything about pumpkins, or weasels, for that matter. I'm just the farm's guard dog now." He rolled over to show the SECURITY sign on his sweater.

"Exactly! Caw. You are the security around here aren't you? Aren't you? Caw."

"All I get to do is bark at you guys every morning. Nuttin' goes on around here. I ain't seen a coyote or fox in months. How would I know the goings on at the Pumpkin Patch?" he asked.

"But the weasels, the weasels! Caw, caw."

"I'll chase the weasels if you want me to. Do ya?"

"Caw, I can't believe anyone can be so dumb? You're the only one I can talk to in this zoo of domesticated dumb, dumb, dumbwits!" Duke cried, covering his eyes with a bent wing.

"Hey wait a minute. What do you mean by 'domesticated dumbwits'?"

"Caw, I'm sorry, but who can we talk to? Someone has to know. Someone has to know."

"Wasn't Patches there? You could ask Patches."

"Caw, oh you oaf! He can't talk. He just stands there shrugging his shoulders! Twirling whirlybirds, scary whirlybirds!"

"I don't know about that, I've seen him move many times!' He paused.

"At least, I think I have. I'm pretty sure I saw him move."

Duke sighed. "Caw, what about Quacks, your farm leader. You do remember Quacks, don't you? The guy who saved you from being put down?"

"'Course I do. He's the officially elected farm patriarch!" Sneezer replied, puffing out his chest. "He's smart!"

"Caw well? Weeeeell?"

"Maybe he just might know what to do. Yup, I'm sure of it." Sneezer nodded and rested his muzzle on his paws again.

"Caw, weeeeeeell? Caw, caw, caw."

"Huh, well what?"

"Are we going to go see Quacks or not! See Quacks or not! Caw, caw."

"Oh. It's after his bedtime so he'll be in the reeds at the duck pond. He's always at the duck pond." Sneezer closed his eyes.

"Well? Weeeeelll? Caw, caw," Duke squawked. He hopped onto Sneezer's shoulders, dug his claws into Sneezer's neck and gave the dog's head three sharp pecks with his black beak. "Is there anybody in there? Caw, in there?"

"Of course, there is. I'm here, aren't I?"

"Quacks, caw," Duke snapped.

"Oh, yeah, you want to go see him. But not now, surely. We can't wake him now. No, no, I don't think he likes being woken up at this time. He's very sensitive about his beauty sleep."

"Caw, beauty sleep, a pig needs beauty sleep? Caw, caw," he mocked. "Caw, let's go, let's go. Wake him up, wake him up."

"Okay. If you think this is that important." Sneezer dragged himself to his arthritic old feet and stretched. "He really did say he wanted his beauty sleep," he protested.

Duke hopped on Sneezer's shoulders and they trotted down the trail toward the duck pond.

"Caw, caw, a pig wanting beauty sleep, caw, caw."

Bruce Kilby

Bruce Kilby

# Chapter 4

# Quacks the Pig

With the nights becoming cooler in the fall, mist formed on the surface of the pond and aimlessly moved across the wet grass on the farm. As it drifted eerily into every corner and dark space, the bushes and trees appeared to come alive. Each bare branch formed into arms with long fingers and the gnarls in the bark changed into hideous faces. With little wind, the mist seemed to take on a life of its own as it slowly floated upward into the night sky as if trying to cover the face of the full moon.

As he travelled down the path, peering at each gruesome expression hidden in the trees, imagining eyes in every shadow, and jumping out of the way each time a branch appeared to reach out to grab him, Sneezer felt most uneasy.

"You didn't pick the best of nights for this, Duke. Nope, not at all. This place is so spooky it's giving me the willies!" he protested. He jumped and swore that something moved when he stared into the spooky woods at eerie shadows. "I don't like this. Not one bit. Not even a little bit. I should be back in my doghouse dreaming of chasing rabbits."

"Caw, you will be in the doghouse forever, if Farmer McSimmons finds all his pumpkins gone. Caw."

"But it's creeeeepy here."

"Caw, some security dog you are! It's October, October, Halloween, around the corner, around the corner, and Sneezer Wheezer is scared! Caw."

Just above their heads, an owl hooted so loudly that Sneezer and even Duke jumped. "Caw, caw!" he squawked, digging his talons deep into Sneezer's back and wrapping both his wings around Sneezer's head, completely covering his eyes. "Caw, scary, so scary, scary, scary, Caw, caw!"

"Yeowoooooh!" Sneezer yelped from the pain between his shoulder blades. He leapt sideways then ran blindly in circles, stumbling head first into a tree trunk.

"Caw. Sorry, so sorry."

"That's the second time you've made me hit my head. Or is it three times? Are you doing that on purpose?"

"Caw. Sorry, so sorry." Releasing his death grip on Sneezer, Duke said, "I see, you can see, scary, yes scary. Caw, caw."

Quickening their pace through the mist covering the trail, they crossed under a turnstile and waded through the tall grass of an open field. Just when they had begun to breathe again, a pheasant flushed out of its nesting spot under their noses. Both Duke and Sneezer cried out in alarm.

"Caw, time to move, time to move," Duke screeched.

"I'm going as fast as I can. I'm not as fast as I used to be."

"Caw faster, faster Caw, caw."

"As fast as these paws will carry me," Sneezer hollered as he wound it up to a full gallop while Duke clung to his back.

As with all hounds, it did not take long before Sneezer started slobbering from his drooping jowls. The more he ran, the more he slobbered. Soon the slimy drool sprayed over his shoulders and splattered

Duke on Sneezer's back. "Caw, caw. Do you mind? Do you mind? I'm getting soaked back here. Keep your goober to yourself!"

"Sorry buddy can't be helped. I'm a drooler!"

"A loser you mean. Loser, loser." Duke covered his face with his wings and held on tight.

The reeds surrounding the pond emerged through the mist as they approached the end of the trail at the water's edge. Relieved they had finally made it Sneezer shook himself in the cold damp air, nearly flinging Duke into the night. Duke's claws clamped down even harder into the baggy skin of Sneezer's back.

"Yipe!" Sneezer cried, glancing over his shoulder. Gobs of drool dripped from from the crow who flapped his wings to shake off the slobber.

"Caw, I suppose you think this funny. Funny!" Duke complained. "Caw, caw, this isn't funny, not funny at all. Caw."

Sneezer rolled on the ground as chuckles rumbled from his belly.

With no summer chorus of croaking frogs and chirping crickets, the silence seemed eerie in the foggy fall night. The pair's protests and amusement faded when they sensed the haunting shadows looming over them.

"Dark, ain't it?" Sneezer muttered, his eyes staring.

"Dark, dark, dark."

Peering into the dark at the still waters edge, they could see nothing.

"What to do, what to do? Caw."

Sneezer had no idea where Quacks might be at this large duck pond—no idea at all. He had never had a reason to come down here and nobody had ever bothered to ask him.

"Quaaaaacks?" Sneezer howled softly into the night. "Quaaaaacks?' a little louder this time. An echo returned from across the pond.

By now, any animal that may have been asleep had surely awakened. Anything that prowled the night also knew where they were. All chirping, croaking, and insect buzzing suddenly stopped. There was dead silence.

For a moment, they listened then Duke said, "Caw, caw, that was well done wasn't it? Well done! Everyone knows we're here! Everyone! Caw."

"Well, we had to try something didn't we? Quaaaaacks?" Sneezer called again then waited, listening. He dared not try to sniff him out in case he sneezed. That would definitely wake up the neighborhood!

"Well that's that, I tried. I guess we can go back to my warm, snuggly dog house now, right?" Sneezer said preparing to leave.

"Caw, caw, no, that won't do. That won't do." Duke gave the dog a sharp peck on the ear.

"Ow…What was that?" Sneezer cried.

"Caw, caw, what? What?"

"Shhhhhhhhhh! Listen!"

A rustling noise came from somewhere to their right side.

"Who goes there?" Sneezer demanded, raising his heckles and assuming his best guard dog pose.

"It's me," said a strange low raspy voice from different direction.

"Who's 'me'?" Sneezer asked pivoting toward the direction of the voice, staring into the darkness. No one answered. Duke tilted his head left then right to listen but heard nothing more.

"Me!" the voice said from directly behind them.

"Whoa!" Sneezer jumped sending Duke fluttering off his back.

"Caw, caw, caw!" Duke squawked.

Before them stood a black-masked, ring-tailed animal. Sneezer recognized the critter at once. He and Farmer McSimmons used to try and hunt this animal on those delightful days before his allergies had set in. He knew they could be vicious if trapped. This one wore a black mask over his black eyes.

"Caw, what are you? What are you?" Duke had never seen this night creature before.

In a low, gravely voice the stranger answered. They call me raccoon but dat's not important. You were making so much noise over here, da boss, er, I mean Quacks sent me to check it out."

"I can understand you," Sneezer said, his heart still pounding.

"Yeah, I learned human speak in the city."

Whoosh! A blur raced by them all and skidded to a stop in a swirl of dust. When the cloud had settled, Sneezer and Duke saw before them a field mouse with big cheeks and a bulging satchel across his shoulder. He also wore a black mask.

"Dat's my partner. He don't talk much," the raccoon explained. "When he does, only I can understand him. He talks so fast most ears can't keep up." Then he cast a sharp glance in Duke's direction. "You crow, keep your eyes off of him. He's Farm Council protected." He stood up straighter. "Whadya doin' 'round these parts anyway?"

"We need to see Quacks, right away. Tonight! Duke here saw something over at the Pumpkin Patch. Something very strange," Sneezer explained.

“At this time of night? You know he…”

“Caw, caw, beauty sleep, beauty sleep.”

“How did he…?”

Duke interrupted. “Something strange, yes sir, yes sir, caw! Got to speak with Quacks, urgent, urgent!”

The raccoon eyed them up and down with his beady, black-masked eyes. “Okay, come on. We’ll take you to see Quacks.” He paused then turned back around, “Wait a minute,” he nodded at his partner, “got to see if you’re packing any heat.”

“Huh,” was all Sneezer was able to say before the mouse raced around his body in a blur. When he stopped, he gave the raccoon a nod. “What do you think I’m carrying under my fur coat, a machine gun?”

The mouse then raced over Duke’s shiny feathers and once again gave a nod toward the raccoon.

“Do you think he might have some arrows attached to the end of those feathers?” Sneezer sneered. “Geesh!”

“You just never know. The Boss needs protection.”

“He’s the farm patriarch not some mafia don!”

“Just doing my job Buddy. Just doing my job,” the raccoon said, wiping his nose with the back of his paw. “Come with me.” He moved off, leading the crew along a narrow overgrown pathway through the reeds.

“This must be the back way,” Sneezer muttered, recalling his tracking days. “There is no way Quacks could fit here.”

It was all Duke could do to hang on to Sneezer’s back as he charged through the tunnel of reeds while cottony seedpods smacked into Duke’s face. Within moments, the reeds parted to reveal a small clearing with a view of the pond. Fireflies danced over the water helping the moon shed light into the dimly lit area, just enough to see Quacks, wearing an admiral's hat, sitting sloppily in a large nest made of reeds and layered with duck down. Duke and Sneezer stared.

"I prefer the nest as a constant reminder of the nests Mildred used to make for me when I was an orphaned babe," Quacks explained, giving Mildred a kindly look. "It calms me so I can think and I sleep better here than I would in any pig sty."

"It sure is better than my doghouse!" Sneezer remarked. "Then again, anything is better than being in the doghouse."

Mildred preened at the water's edge, glancing fondly at Quacks. Taking down from her undercoat, she tucked it along the edges of the nest.

"As you can see, I am just getting ready for bed," Quacks said. "Aw, thanks mom! Nothing's more comfy than a down mattress." He shifted his round rump, searching for just the right spot then plopping down. "What brings you here my friends?"

"Those guys frisked us!" Sneezer glared at the raccoon and the field mouse.

"Caw, caw. He ruffled my feathers! Ruffled my feathers! Caw, caw." Duke bobbed his head as he spat seeds from his beak.

"Oh, don't worry about him. He came here some months ago from the big city. He got caught in a pound round up while stealing eggs!"

Every duck, goose, and swan in the area snapped their heads round and glared at the raccoon, upon which the raccoon ducked his head and backed into the reeds grinning sheepishly. The fat cheeked mouse followed closely behind him.

"He might be a little rough around the edges but believe me, he learned his lesson when he got caught in the roundup," Quacks declared making sure all the birds had heard.

"He got the wits scared out of him when they caged him next to two escaped Dobermans," Quacks explained to Duke and Sneezer in a hushed voice. "He thought he was a goner but his life was spared and he was brought out into the country on some 'relocation' program'." Quacks called after the raccoon. "He knows if he gets caught again it will be back in the slammer...or something much, much worse!" Quacks dragged a hoof across his throat in a cutting motion.

The raccoon peered through the tall grasses and blinked slowly, faking a pout.

"Okay, tell me what happened Duke?"

"Caw, you hear what I say? What I say?"

"Yes, I understand beast and fowl."

"Caw, caw. Strange, very strange. Caw, I was flying, yes, flying, over to Raptor Ridge heading for a midnight feed. Yes, midnight feed. Caw, caw."

"Yes."

"Caw, going to get potato sticks from the humans, potato sticks. Humans nesting in the metal killing beasts."

"Yes, yes, get on with it."

"Caw, I don't know why they press their faces together in the metal monster. Press faces. Regurgitate. Regurgitate food for their chicks? Don't know, Caw!"

"Get to with the strange part," Quacks demanded.

"Caw, caw, pumpkins were moving. Pumpkins were moving in the Pumpkin Patch, caw."

"Moving you say. Are you sure this is before you ate? You didn't eat something that was a little off, did you? Some rotten pizza or deep fried onion ring from the dumpster perhaps? Something that upset your tummy could have affected your eyes."

"No food, no time, no time. Hungry, hungry."

"But I've never seen or heard of pumpkins moving before."

"Caw, no, no. The weasels were stealing them. The weasels stealing them! Caw, caw, caw." He bobbed his whole body up and down, desperate for somebody to believe him.

"Oh, now that is interesting. Very interesting, indeed. Weasels don't eat pumpkins, do they?"

Sneezer shrugged.

"Why would weasels want pumpkins?" Quacks mused. "And where were they taking them?" Blank stares answered him back.

"Scared them, I did, scared them I did. Dropped the pumpkins, dropped the pumpkins, they did." Duke explained.

"Me n' Pronts have seen a lot more weasels in da area lately and I don't know why," said the masked stranger still lurking in the reeds.

"Caw, lots and lots."

"Do you want us to check things out Boss?" the raccoon asked in his heavy city accent, rubbing his nose on the back of his paw.

"Don't call me Boss! Call me Quacks like I told you, especially in front of the farm animals!"

"Yes, Boss. I mean, yes Quacks."

Quacks seemed satisfied then, nodding toward the raccoon and the field mouse, he said, "All right, that's a good idea. We definitely need to find out what's going on. You two go over to the Pumpkin Patch and find out what you can. Stand watch all night with Patches if you have to."

The raccoon and field mouse looked at each other. "Who is Patches?" rasped the raccoon.

"He's the scarecrow in the patch. See if those sneaky varmints come back to the field. They must want pumpkins for something." The raccoon and field mouse turned to leave. "Those weasels can be pretty vicious, so if you see them, keep out of sight. And don't try to stop them or they'll tear you to pieces for just looking at them. Just see where they go."

"Okay Boss, um, I mean Quacks." The raccoon and field mouse disappeared through the reeds and into darkness, silent as shadows.

"Who is that masked mammal anyway?" Sneezer asked then added, "Why would a raccoon wear a mask anyway?"

"Nobody really knows his name. He just showed up one day, all alone. He said he had to keep his new identity a secret and couldn't tell us his real name so we just call him Stranger."

"I'm not sure if I want to trust a lone stranger wearing a mask!" Sneezer sniffed.

"Well, he's been good to me and the farm. He can reach a little farther than the arms of farm justice if you know what I mean."

"Caw, caw, the rat, the rat!"

"That's no rat, that's his sidekick Pronto!"

"Caw, rat to me, rat to me!"

"He's a field mouse who loves sunflower seeds. He always stores a few in his cheeks. That's why they are so fat. He leaves a trail of spits everywhere. His murse is full of them."

"Murse?"

"Yeah, don't call it a purse. He gets mad. He calls it a murse."

"How did Stranger and Pronto hook up?'

"They met in the hay fields one day just after Stranger got here. Stranger was down and out and near starvation. Being a city raccoon, he was used to stealing or begging off gullible humans who would feed him because they thought he was cute." Quacks rolled his eyes. "He wasn't used to farmers and their fire sticks taking shots at him. He never learned to hunt in the wild. Pronto brought him to the farm and fed him on some of Daisy's spilt milk, barley from the silo, and some trout out of McSimmons' catch. After that, they became best of friends and partners. That's why Pronto wears a mask, too."

"Aha! So that's where those fishes went," Sneezer exclaimed. "I got blamed for that theft. Tied up to the doghouse...again!" Sneezer complained. "Whenever anything that goes missing around here, Sneezer get's tied to the doghouse!" he muttered.

"Oh, by the way, you're wasting your time trying to listen to Pronto," Quacks added ignoring Sneezer's complaints. "Stranger is the only one who can understand him because he talks way too fast, even for me. Now Duke," Quacks continued, "I want you to fly over the Patch again. See what you can see. Keep your eyes peeled. You never know...they may come back again. Warn Stranger and Pronto if you see anything."

With a nod, Duke lifted off into the night air.

"Sneezer, you go back to the house and make sure Farmer McSimmons hasn't woken up. In the morning, make sure he doesn't go to the Patch, just in case. Act like nothing has happened."

"Okay, that should be easy." Sneezer turned and crept off quietly back through the reeds to his doghouse alone, eyes wide and ears on alert.

In the silence, Quacks began to ponder aloud. "Duke is right, there is indeed something strange going on. We'll have to get to the bottom of this." Then he yawned and looked at Mildred whose beak was nuzzled under her wing and sound asleep. "Well, it's late and time for us to get some shut-eye. We have things to do tomorrow." Quacks nestled down and waved his hoof to scatter the fireflies, leaving only the moon to light the way for Stranger, Pronto, Sneezer, and Duke.

Bruce Kilby

# Chapter 5

# The Witch and Weasels

Deep in the dark, damp woods there sat a rundown, old hunters cottage nestled amongst the twisting, moss-covered roots of a huge, ancient, gnarled oak tree. It had been there for a very long time. The slate roof had several tiles missing or loose; same with stones from the river rock chimney. The plaster and timber walls were cracked and covered with mildew. Rubbed spots on the dirty windows showed that someone had at least attempted to look outside at one time. The cracks in the doors would not hold out the cold should a harsh winter set in or the winds of fall begin to howl but they kept strangers out.

A cackling scream burst from a shabby black-robed witch hunched over her caldron. "What do you mean, you didn't get the pumpkins!" A band of cowering weasels backed away from her. She paced like a lone wolf around the large metal pot as if prowling on a hunt. "I want those pumpkins! I must have those pumpkins!" Curling her boney fingers into fists and raising them into the air, she spun and glared at the trembling weasels. "My Hallowe'en cannot happen without those pumpkins! Do you hear me! You good-for-nothing pack of poor excuses who call yourselves thieves!"

Mordred, the witch's black cat now terrified scuttled off to a safe hiding perch on the windowsill. Having been the victim of the witch's wrath before, he wanted no part of this.

"But, but your great witchness, we, we were seen! One of the Skysquawkers saw us," stammered Sleazel, the lead weasel. The deathlike gray-green face of the witch towered over him.

"Do you think I'm stupid? Everyone knows that crows never fly at night!" the witch shrieked.

"Of course not, your evil highness. We would never think.... you, stupid," he squeaked. "I mean..."

"Get on with it!" she demanded.

"We didn't think they flew at night either but there he was, eye poking black beak n' all!" said Meazel, the spotted weasel. "The other animals call him Duke."

"He came right out of the dark! All of a sudden-like. He started squawking like a screeching ghost!" Sleazel added.

"Oh, you quivering cowards! You're a shame to your own kind," she hissed as Mordred looked on from his perch, calmly licking a paw. For once somebody else would feel her wrath. He began to purr.

The witch grabbed a ladle by the big open fireplace and stirred a foul smelling orange and green goop boiling in her cauldron. "My stupid rats could have done better than you lot! What do you think I should do with these poor excuses?" the witch asked her purple-cloaked husband, the Weasel Warren Warlock.

In a far corner of the room, a large dark form crouched at an ancient table scattered with scrolls and symbolic charts. The table dripped with from the numerous candles lit around the desk.

"My darling Evilla, you could always boil them!" he remarked, barely lifting up his eyes from studying an ancient witchcraft tome so old that the pages looked as though they would fall apart at the slightest breath of wind.

"Yes, my sweet, boiled weasel. How interesting," she mused. "Weasel stew can be very tasty with some wing of bat and eye of goat. I especially like the idea of wolverine tongue salted with weasel eyeballs!" he added casually turning another page.

The weasels gasped.

He sighed. "But it must be served with skunk cabbage and raw leeks and those garlic butter slugs. You know I must have my vegetables." Turning back to his work, he lazily rubbed his fingers together and a strange blue light glowed from his long fingernail. Once lit, he casually flicked the blue bolt toward a candlewick. It instantly flashed into flame. He unrolled another scroll. "And you would look so lovely with a new fur collar around your cloak, would you not, my pretty?"

"Tempting, very tempting indeed, my dear, dear Dreadmore. You are so thoughtful. Unfortunately, I need these scrawny vermin."

Her voice changed from sweet to nasty. "We have a contract, don't we boys?" she whined with a sneer. The cowering weasels huddled, shivering. "And we know what happens to little weasels who try to...weasel out their contract, don't we, boys?"

With caps in hand and beads of sweat dripping off their brows the weasels nodded.

"I have to have all of Weasel Warren's pumpkins so I can put together my little, shall we say, All Hallows Eve surprise!" she cackled hysterically. "My beautiful surprise indeed!  Heh, heh, heh. You wouldn't want to spoil my little surprise now would you little one?" she growled, ruffling the fur on Sleazel's neck with a filthy, pointed fingernail.

"Er, no, no, of course not, Your Witchness." At the cold touch of the witch's fingers stroking the nape of his neck Sleazel felt quite faint. "I, I, wouldn't want to spoil nuttin', Your Evilness."

Mordred jumped down from the window and started to rub himself around the witch's legs, purring in agreement.

"How can I make my Hallowe'en a delectable fright night without all of the pumpkins? Our night, the one night a year where evil gets its chance to play and all the children of the world make Hallo...weenie of it!" Her pitch rose even higher. "Cutesy ballerina tutus, purple dragons with no teeth, and fairy costumes! Can you believe it? Fairies! Our mortal enemies! I can't stand it!" she howled, storming around the room again.

To Sleazel's relief, she picked up Mordred and cradled him in her arms, giving him a scratch behind the ear. "And if I see another Batman, Spiderman, or, or Superman costume, I'll scream! Heros? We don't need no stinking heros! We need…we need…villains!"

Now completely enraged, she flung the startled cat aside and stretched her arms once more. Forked lightning bolts sparked from her fingertips, flying in all directions around the room. "I want evilness to return to my beloved Hallowe'en! It is our last night to play and I love to play. Don't I my dearest?"

"Of course, you do, my dear. We love playing our little tricks." The warlock glanced up half amused then resumed his meditation on a scroll.

"Our little tricks!" she sneered, "I mean real tricks! I want ghouls and ghosts, ogres and orcs, vampires and werewolves to roam once more! I want humans to smell fear, afraid of the night, and to huddle together in their puny little homes to shake in their boots! And when we say, 'Trick or treat,' they will learn we prefer tricks! I prefer nasty little tricks like turning them into toads or giving them warts!"

The warlock clapped his hands in agreement. "Yes, my sweet. It is our turn and we don't play around. Do we, my dear?"

"I prefer eating their cats than their sweet tidbits! Chocolate bars, chips, candy apples and sweets? Yeuck!" She paused. "And for these disgusting little children! I want them to hide under their beds hoping we don't find them. I want them afraid we will come and eat them! I want the hour of the witch to come once more!" she screamed hysterically. "And, of course...warlocks, too." She smiled toward her nodding husband.

"G-g-give us another chance, Your Great Evilness," Sleazel stuttered. "We will get them somehow." His knees shaking so badly that his teeth rattled. "Maybe he's gone by now. We'll go back, okay? We'll go back and get the pumpkins this very minute, oh Great Witchness."

"You had better, you cowardly, skulking, conniving, flea-bitten vermin!" she howled. "Eye of Weasel is very useful in my 'Slink of Night' spell!" she glared once more. "Do you understand me? Do YOU?"

The room darkened and her eyes glowed bright red. Outside, dark clouds as if summoned, a flash of lightning burst through the windows and with a crack of thunder her shadow loomed over the shaking weasels. Slowly, they backed toward the door in absolute terror.

Mordred panicked and ran to hide under the table to spit and hiss.

Meazel tripped over Diezel, the black weasel, in his haste to back up. Sleazel stood frozen to the floor, eyes staring. "Y-y-yes, my Enchanted Darkness of Evilness. I m-m-mean, my witchness, I m-m-mean, Your Witchness!"

Pointing a long, boney finger at the weasels, she calmly added, "If you lazy excuses for thieves do not get me my pumpkins, your days as fur bearing, long-tailed rats are numbered. Do I make myself clear?"

The three of them nodded in unison.

"Now get out of here before I change my mind!" She raised her arm and with as much force she could muster, threw the cauldron ladle at the scurrying weasels scrambling to squeeze through the crack at the bottom of the Witch of Weasel Warren's front door.

Dreadmore looked up from his scrolls with a sinister grin. "I believe you have their attention, my dear."

Mordred came out of hiding to chase the weasels with a clawed paw swatting at them through a crack in the door. Outside, the other weasels in the gang, who had stacked themselves one on top of another with ears pressed tightly to the door, had listened to every word said inside.

As Sleazel, Meazel, and Diezel squeezed out through the crack they yelled, "Run!" just as the ladle handle splintered through a gap in the door and wedged itself in, vibrating. The stack of weasels tumbled a fumbling, bumbling pile of fur.

"Ruuuuunn!" cried another, as they tumbled over each other in their mad haste to get away. Mordred's evil eye peered out from the bottom of the door as they scattered into the darkness.

As the scrambling weasels regrouped some distance from the ramshackle woodcutter's house, Sleazel stopped. "We're in big trouble now, boys!" he said, panting as they scampered through the Northwoods forest.

"Come on gang! We have to get those pumpkins!"

Bruce Kilby

# Chapter 6

# The Night Watch

The early morning mist lying low over the Pumpkin Patch drifted mysteriously around the solitary orange balls scattered over the ghostly setting. Looking like gravestones, damp dew clung and dripped down the sides of each orb giving them an eerie sheen under the pale moonlight. A distant owl's hoot was all that broke the silence in the pitch black of night as Stranger and Pronto crept through the entrance gate of McSimmons' pumpkin patch.

Sounding like a sped up DJ turntable, Pronto nervously blurted, "I really don't like this, Stranger, no don't like it at all. Really scary here, we should be in our nests, yes sir, shouldn't be here! Danger, danger, Stranger. Stranger?"

Stranger hushed him. "Mute the mug, I'm trying to get da lay of da land here. Can't think with you flapping your gums!"

He sniffed around the ground and in the air trying to pick up scents. He checked the many footprints in the soft, recently tilled earth and found a few pumpkin stalks that had been chewed and the loose pumpkins chaotically dropped in the weasels' frantic scramble to escape the gaze of Duke Skysquawaker.

"Now what have we got here?" he said under his breath. "The stench of those sleazy vermin burns my sniffer!" Stranger stood on his haunches and stared into the darkness toward the woods. "They were here all right and not too long ago. Looks like they went that-a-way." He stretched a gnarled paw in the direction of the Northwoods. Peering into the blackness, even he, with a raccoon's nocturnal vision, saw no movement—nothing at all.

Pronto climbed up on top of Stranger's head for a better look but he saw nothing either.

"I got a sneaky feelin' they're 'round here real close. Pronts, take a lap around da patch 'n' see if anyone's out dere," Stranger ordered.

Pronto's eyes bulged. "What? Me? I'm not goin' out there, not me! It's scary out there. Why don't you take a 'lap around the patch'?"

"'Cause you're the bullet and I'm the gun. Now git goin'."

"It's always me—check this, check that, run here, run there," he mumbled as he ambled off.

"Ain't you gone yet?" Stranger growled.

"I'm going, I'm going."

Pronto crawled up on top of one of McSimmons' big, prized pumpkins and sniffed the air in all directions. He even looked up in the air in case an owl was out there seeking a midnight snack. A field mouse is the target of many predators and he knew he needed to keep a sharp eye out at all times. Can't be too careful, he thought, sensing no one about.

He dashed off so fast his furry little body became only a blur ripping through the patch. When he thought it safe, he skidded to a stop and sniffed the air again. Then off he went, up and over, under and around pumpkins, checking for weasels or any other kind of spooky prowler.

Concerned for his buddy, Stranger strained his sharp gaze into the night after Pronto but seconds later and out of breath, Pronto tumbled to a skidding stop next to Stranger.

"No one here," he gasped making stranger jump.

"Whoa, dat was fast!" he said gathering himself. "See anything?"

"Just the scarecrow and he's not sayin' much. It felt eerie in the north corner near the woods. I could sense something. In fact, I got goose bumps all over my goose bumps!"

"Yeah, I got the same feelin'. Couldn't see nuttin' though. By da way, da scarecrows name's Patches. He don't look like much but it looks like Patches dere has da best view of de patch from that rise in the middle of da field. Come on, Pronts, let's set up under dat long coat of his."

"Are you sure about that?" Pronto asked, looking at the ominous outline backlit by the moon.

"Come on li'l buddy, it's safer under dere where we won't be sittin' ducks and no one can see us."

Still not convinced, Pronto bolted after Stranger toward the tall, raggedy, straw-stuffed scarecrow standing his lonely night vigil in the centre of the field.

The foreboding statue wore a long, well-used coat with patches on both elbows, on the left shoulder, and over a torn pocket. At the end of his straw stuffed outstretched arms, he was clad in a worn pair of motorcycle gloves, one of which held a rusty scythe. A ratty Fedora hat, strangely similar to the one Farmer McSimmons always wore, sat on his head. The head was made from straw stuffed into an old grain sack with black buttons sewn on for eyes. Someone had also stitched him a toothless grin and an X for a nose using binder twine. Whirlybirds on each shoulder stood motionless in the damp, cool October night. Patches was not much to look at but he did his job keeping the birds away even if he couldn't move.

"Looks like he's been stuck here for a while," observed Pronto.

"Yup. I hope he don't come alive while he has dat scythe in his hands," Stranger answered. "He looks like the Grim Reaper!"

After several silent moments had passed, Pronto whispered, "It sure is quiet. I can hear you breathing."

"I ain't used to it," Stranger whispered back. "The big city had sirens goin' all night. Never a moment's peace but you get used to it. But dis? Dis is too quiet." He looked up at the sky. "And look at all dem stars. Never see dat many in de city."

A few moments later a slight breeze picked up and the whirlybirds on Patches shoulders fluttered and started turning.

Stranger sniffed the air again. "Weasels always smell guilty of something," he mumbled. "I can smell 'em, like cats can smell fish bones a hundred yards away. I know they're near. I just know it."

They scurried for cover in the darkness under the opening of Patches' long coat and peered out from the gap in the flap.

After a few tense moments, Pronto squeaked, "I hear something."

"I hear it, too."

"It's coming from behind us."

"Okay, buster, who else is in here?" Stranger turned around, searching the darkness under Patches' coat.

"Is that...is that you?" said a strange voice.

"Dat voice, I've heard dat voice before," Stranger replied. "And dat smell?"

"It is me!" the voice answered with pride.

"Punko Stinkola? Hey, Pronts, dis is Punko Stinkola or Stinkerola or somethin' like dat. He's from da big city. We used to hang out together in da alleys and back lanes. You know, shared a few meals from garbage cans and dumpsters. Did a few jobs together, if ya know what I mean."

"No, no, no signore, not Punko Stinkerola. Soft 'c', soft 'c'. My name is Punce Stincattio my friend. My family is many generations from Naples, Italia. Mario, don of the Stincattio family, came to this country to set up businesses in the forties, if you know what I mean." The visitor's eyebrow wiggled up and down.

"We both got caught up in the dragnets," Stranger explained. "No matter which way we ran, da pound had us surrounded. Sirens were everywhere. Still don't know how they knew we were there. Anyway, we travelled on da same relocation bus out here. We thought we were on half a car ride, if you know what I mean."

Being a field mouse from the country, Pronto had no idea what they meant. He frowned at Stranger.

"You know, out to some desolate spot where dey gives you a shovel to dig your own final, shall we say, resting spot?"

"Yeah, yeah, so when they opened the cages, we all took off in all directions just as we had planned on the trip out," the visitor added. "We thought they couldn't catch us all if we scattered. I haven't seen this little fella or any of the others since."

"We call him Punk the Skunk," Stranger said with a grin.

Now that a sliver of moonlight shone through a gap in the coat, Pronto could see that this skunk was not like any country skunk he knew.

This one was pure white with a black stripe down the middle of his back. He wore a New York Nicks skaters hat turned backwards and several gold chains around his neck. A diamond-encrusted dollar sign adorned the longest one.

In his usual friendly country way, Pronto spat in his tiny paw then thrust toward the skunk. "Pleasure to meet you, Punce Sti, Stina…nattio"

"Don't worry about dat, Pronts. No one else could say his name either so we in the business used to call him Punk de Skunk. Right, Punk?"

"*Si.* If you say so." He shrugged with a sigh. "Nevertheless, it is so good to see a friendly face again." He gave Stranger a high, a low five, a middle finger wiggle topped off with a paw slide across each other's palms. "I have not seen any of our old friends from the city either."

"Yeah, they scattered us all over da place. Didn't want us to get back together or find our way back to da city. Rumors in da pound said we were gonna be lab rats. They did somethin' to me, I know. Experiments, if ya know what I mean."

"Ya, me too. They stuck me with a pin thing, them the next thing I know, I'm not sure I'm a boy no more. They called it muter, neuter or somethin' like that." The skunk shivered.

"All I remember was seein' bright lights, then waking up in my cage. By de way, Punk, dis is Pronto. Pronto, dis is Punk, the Skunk."

Pronto bowed and squeaked. The skunk understood the tone of the mouse's greeting.

"How did you meet Mack the Rac...?"

In a flash, Stranger covered Punk's mouth with both paws. "No, no dat ain't me no more. Dey gave me a new identity and no one is to know

I'm here, see. They call me Stranger around dese parts. Anyone finds out my true name, I'm a goner, especially from de old gang. It was part of da deal when I testified on de egg caper."

"Oh, it was you who ratted them all out!"

"Yeah, but dey said dey wouldn't put anyone down if I talked. If I didn't do what they asked, dey said dey would hunt us all down and put us in da pound. And you know what dat means." He slashed a paw across his throat from ear to ear.

Pronto gulped.

"Si, signore. I wondered why I didn't see anyone around no more. They caught me tagging. You know a little spray here, a little spray there." He grinned and wiggled his behind.

"Oh, I ain't surprised you weren't caught before. After you fell into dat chemical vat, you weren't no normal skunk. I could handle dat. But now you reek! Whew, dat disgusting scent you spray. It's toxic! Turns everything green, including me!"

Pronto was quite used to the smell of skunks from the country but now he held his nose, rolled his eyes up into his head, and flopped to the floor.

"Yeah, you got it. But Punk the Skunk is a master. He can clear a room in a heartbeat. It lasts for days and days. Couldn't do it in da park, no, had to do it everywhere we was. In da alleys, in front of restaurants and even da bakery didn't smell of fresh bread no more! You know how I likes the smell of fresh bread! The one and only, Punk da Skunk!"

Punk grinned. "Well, I had to claim my territory. Any blank space would do but never where some other artist had tagged before. No, no, signore, only empty spaces."

"No wonder dey hunted you down."

"I like to share my talents."

"Well don't do it around here. I want to smell dem comin'."

"Who would that be signore?"

"Da weasels," he said in a low raspy voice.

"WEASELS! Show me where they are, I'll tag 'em right here, right now!" Punk said bravely turning his rear to the gap in the old coat.

"No, no we don't want to be discovered. We're keepin' six."

"You're just watchin' out, signore?"

"Yeah, dats it. When dey come back we want to see what dey are doin' and den follow 'em."

"Okay, signore," said the skunk. He moved back from the front flap, settled himself and, to Stranger's relief, relaxed his tail.

Stranger caught a whiff in the air. "D'ya smell dat?"

"It wasn't me," Punk whispered immediately.

"No, no dat?"

"No? You know that I cannot smell a thing." Pronto started to giggle.

"Nor would you if you tagged like me. I can barely smell my own!"

"I think da weasels are coming?" Pronto leapt to his feet, now on full alert.

Suddenly, Duke flew in under the back flap of Patches' coat, his feathers ruffled. He couldn't enter from the scarecrow's front because with the scythe, whirlybirds, and Farmer McSimmons' hat, Patches terrified him.

"Caw, they're coming! They're coming! Caw, caw."

"Shhh, lower your voice," Stranger cried, startled. "I don't wanna get caught by a pack of weasels. You can fly; we can't." Whispering, Stranger asked, "From which direction?"

"Caw, from the Northwoods, Northwoods, caw." Duke raucous voice was difficult to muffle.

Peering out from beneath Patches' long coat, Stranger focused his night vision toward the Northwood.

"I can see 'em comin' all right. Sneaking in like a bad smell. Yup, like a bad smell."

"Did you just...?" Pronto glanced over his shoulder at Punk.

"No! That's them!" the skunk retorted, pointing out into the darkness.

"Oh believe me," Stranger insisted, "if it was him, you would know! Dis is definitely weasel."

Like an army of soldier ants making their way through the jungles of Africa, the weasels once again began lifting the pumpkins and marching back out of the patch under a broken fence rail, the same way they had came in.

A long line of pumpkins appeared to effortlessly glide across the field. They pulled tiny carts and pushed wheelbarrows to load up with pumpkins. Some pumpkins were so heavy that even two or three weasels struggled to carry them. Others were hurriedly gnawing on the stems of new pumpkins while others rolled them in position ready to be carried away.

"Come on, boys. Put your backs into it. We got to have all these pumpkins out and back again by morning!" ordered Sleazel.

"Take 'em out den bring 'em back? Dat's odd," Stranger whispered.

"Why would they need to do that?" Pronto asked as he poked his head out further for a better view.

"Dunno. Well, dey're taking 'em somewhere. I think we'll hafta follow deese varmints and see where dey go." He glanced down at his tiny companion who was vehemently shaking his head in disagreement. "Oh, come on buddy," Stranger assured Pronto, "we won't get caught."

Pronto ran in a circle under the coat, faking stabbing himself. Then he flopped on the ground as though dead.

Ignoring the warning, Stranger ordered, "Pronts, you go ahead of the line and see which direction dey take. Don't let 'em see ya. I'll follow up de rear to make sure dey don't make any sudden turns or split up."

"Okay, boss," Pronto obeyed.

Stranger looked for the crow but in the pitch darkness he couldn't make him out. "Duke, you'd better go back. You know what happened last time dey saw you."

"Caw, caw; good, good." Duke's voice rasped out of the blackness.

"What about him?" Pronto squeaked, tilting his head toward the Punk.

"Ya wanna get in on dis for old times' sake?" Stranger asked his old pal.

"No, no, no signore. Believe me as much as I would like to, I need to get back to the city somehow. I must get back to the family. As the successor in line to be the next Don, I have to make sure that another family doesn't try to muscle in on our business, yes?" His face became troubled. "They are like crows. As soon as they think you're down and it's safe, they come in to pick at the bones." Suddenly, he realized that Duke was glaring at him. "Er, present company excluded, of course. My humble apologies, signore."

"Okay, it's up to you then, Pronts." Stranger nudged the mouse with his elbow, then turning back to his city friend he continued, "Dere's a farm close by where you can get some rest. I know de boss and he won't mind if you hang for a couple of days before you make de long trip back. By de way, how do you know which way to go?"

"I have a skunk's nose for intuition, signore."

"Dat's good 'cause it ain't no good for anything else! Take care old friend."

"Ciao!" Punk said with a wink as he slipped out the back of the scarecrow's coat.

Stranger and Pronto glided out through the front opening of Patches' overcoat and slipped into the night shadows going separate ways.

Duke followed Punk out the back way then hopped until he was behind the rise before he unfolded his wings and took flight.

Using the cover of darkness and the shadows of the pumpkins, the masked duo moved silently through the tangle of vines toward the snaking line of weasels. Darting from one pumpkin to the next, Pronto sped to the front of the weasels' line while Stranger held back to cover the rear.

Behind them, a strange blue aura spread over Patches. He began to shudder as though he wanted to follow but he could not move.

The long line of pumpkins silently trailed out of the patch like the slow moving wagon trains that had once travelled west on the Oregon

Trail. Outriders made sure the procession stayed safe and more importantly, undetected. Under the cover of darkness and the low-lying mist, they crept deep into the forest.

"What was that?" Meazel blurted in a hushed voice as he felt something or someone whiz past him.

"What was what?" Diezel answered as he pranced back and forth on the left flank of the orange train.

"That!" he said spinning his head as he felt a fresh gush of wind pass him once again.

"Ahh, it's nuttin'; just the wind. Keep your eyes peeled."

"Seemed to me like somethin', or someone, was out there. This mist is giving me the creeps."

Diezel sniffed the wind and curled his lip. "I can't smell nuttin', not even a field mouse. It's just the shadows of the forest spooking you. Your eyes must be playin' tricks. Get back to work."

The weasel gang members struggled with the large oddly shaped squashes, heaving them across logs, streams, slopes, and through the deep bracken. As they tracked deeper into the forest, one of the wheelbarrows lost its front wheel while they were crossing a small stream when it jammed between two rocks. Immediately, several weasels dropped what they were carrying and jumped in the water, ran to the breakdown and heaved up the side of the loaded wheelbarrow while others struggled to put the wheel back on. With so many helpers, the repair didn't take long and soon they were moving again. But the little group had now fallen behind the main caravan.

Suddenly Sleazel appeared. "Hey, you guys! Pick up the pace. You're lagging behind! We gotta keep movin'."

"Ya, boss," Meazel growled.

"And make sure no one's following us," Sleazel ordered. "I got a weird feeling about this one, lads. That Duke Skysquawker bird caught us earlier, so make sure it don't happen again."

"Right, boss."

Meazel and Deizel cracked their whips."Her almighty witchness will have our hides if we get caught again. And I ain't gonna be the one wrapped around her neck as her new fur collar," Diezel snarled. "You got it?!"

"Okay, we got it, your sleaziness. I'm on it like a hawk, like a hawk," replied Beazel eyeing the night sky. Greazel's and Teazel's heads swiveled left and right, now on high alert.

Stranger had heard every word from his hiding place in a nearby hollow log. "Heh, heh, heh," he muttered under his breath, "those dimwits wouldn't know if a herd of buffalo was following them." Then he licked his paws, washed his face, and quietly slipped back into the shadows.

Bruce Kilby

Bruce Kilby

# Chapter 7

# A Potion in Motion

By the time the front edge of the column reached the clearing where the Witch of Weasel Warren's cottage stood, the moon had begun its descent over the western edge of the forest.

"We have them," Sleazel said as they entered the filthy hovel. "We have the pumpkins, your witchness."

"It certainly took you scoundrels long enough!" the witch bellowed as she stood bending over her cauldron. "Come! We don't have a lot of time. The brew is almost ready and I don't want it to spoil." From a wooden spoon, she sniffed then tasted, then lifted her eyes toward the ceiling as she relished the tang of the putrid brew.

"Coming along nicely," she announced.

The weasels crowded just inside the door where a mere whiff of the boiling concoction's caustic smell burned their eyes and made them gasp for breath.

Ignoring them, Evilla turned her attention to a list written on a piece of ratty-edged old parchment. She checked off each ingredient. "Now let me see, a phantom's foot, yes; ghoul's tongue, jaws of a werewolf, yes; vampire blood, yes, yes." She hesitated, "but I taste...something missing."

She rummaged through her shelves picking up vials and squinting at their contents. "Hmmm, now what is it? Gypsy tears? I don't think so," she mumbled. "It's something more evil...what could it be?"

"Don't forget a witch's mole!" reminded Dreadmore. He twitched his magicians' staff, changing his raven, which was tied to a perch with a long chain, into a long-eared hare. "No, no, that's not it," he murmured, turning his attention back to the scrolls spread out before him. "How do I do that spell again? I'll remember it I know I will."

"Yes, my dear. That's it!" Evilla cried. "A witches mole, it is!"

She briefly considered cutting off one of her own moles then thought better of it. She grabbed the set of keys that hung on a long silver chain around her neck. Using one of the small keys she unlocked an old chest sitting on the table and reached inside it for an old curio box. As if picking up a grain of salt, from inside the box she plucked a tiny black hairy growth.

"And one witches mole."

With a final little plink, she stirred the pungent, unpalatable sludge into syrupy goo. The brew's steam broiled over the cauldron sides and turned from a sickening lime green hue to an eerie dark purple.

"Now that's what I'm talking about!" She inhaled deeply. "Mmmmmm, sooooo goood!"

When the newly produced, nasty acrid stench reached the sensitive noses of the nearby weasels they promptly began to gag, splutter, and choke. Even Mordred coughed as if he were spitting up a fur ball. Dreadmore didn't even flinch.

"Oh, don't be such weasel weenies!" the witch snapped. "This potion is an elixir, a most wonderful confectionery. A manna, you might say," she gushed.

"Is it ready, my love?"

"Ready," she replied, "Now we can start dipping the pumpkins!"

Pronto had crept in unnoticed through the crack in the front door where the ladle had wedged a few hours earlier. He climbed the leg of a stool and crawled up behind Deazel who was totally engrossed in the witches conjuring. After making sure no one would notice, he jumped and scampered up the raggedy curtains then leapt onto a dusty rafter supporting the roof. From up there, he could observe and hear everything.

Unfortunately, it didn't take long before the odor of the purple concoction wafted up to him. His eyes began to water and he covered his mouth with his paws so as not to wretch and give his position away.

"Eeeyuck! " he exclaimed, muffled as he gagged. Along with the weasels, he too held his breath. It didn't take long before he slowly turned red then blue, then purple, until he could hold his breath no longer.

"Wheeew." His breath escaped in a gasp. All heads in the room snapped toward the direction of the eruption.

"Get him!" Sleazel shouted, pointing in Pronto's direction. A sudden frenzy of weasel fur hurtled after Pronto from every direction.

Pronto scurried along the rafter beams darting alone one route after another. As the weasels blocked his path from in front and behind, he gathered his courage and took a daring leap from a beam to the chain of the ceiling lantern, then from there to another rafter. Narrowly avoiding the gnashing teeth of more weasels closing in, he scooted first this way then that until finally he sped around a corner on a plate shelf and came to a screeching halt.

He was face to face with the green eyes of Mordred the cat.

His ponderous body ready pounce, Mordred's eyes narrowed and he smiled a devilish grin. If he caught the mouse, he would earn a rare pampering scratch from his evil mistress. He mewled and flicked his tail back and forth. Just as he was to pounce, Pronto sprayed him like a machine gun with the sunflower seeds stored in his cheeks. Mordred blinked and Pronto ran up and over the now astonished cat's head, down his back, and somersaulted off his tail. As he ran, he crammed handfuls of fresh sunflower seeds into his cheeks from his satchel.

The stunned cat snarled a long nasally whine and whipped around, claws flashing as he swiped at thin air.

Pronto's speed caused complete mayhem in the cottage. The weasels scampered this way and that, up and down, over and under, and round and round. Many of them ran into, tripped, or knocked over each other, and the furniture, in their attempt to capture one tiny mouse.

Pots flew, jars tipped, chairs reeled, and candles snuffed. Even the witch and warlock's magic brooms got into the action swatting at Pronto but instead, nailed some of the slow-dodging weasels. Bodies flew everywhere, as the room dissolved into total pandemonium.

"STOOOOOOP!" The Witch of Weasel Warren, gripping the handle of her cauldron.

As if an instant ice age had fallen upon the hut, everyone froze dead in his or her tracks. Weasels halted in mid-stride while others crashed to the floor in mid-leap. The brooms clattered to the floor while Mordred scrambled for cover under a cupboard. Not a peep could be heard until one remaining plate, spinning on the spot, wobbled then tipped over and smashed onto the floor.

"It's just a mouse, you fools!" the witch cried. "You're not scared of one little teensy, weensy mouse are you? You big, brave, nasty weasels?"

The weasels looked at each other in stunned silence.

She changed from sarcastic to demanding, "Now let's get on with it. We don't have all night!"

Scared out of his wits, Pronto had scampered out the window next to the backdoor. He was moving so fast he misjudged the ledge. He soared through the air, falling as he flew. He closed his eyes, preparing for the pain when he hit the ground. For what seemed an eternity he fell...straight into Strangers arms. When he realized he was not hurt, he opened one eye and looked around.

"Dat was close. Are you all right little buddy?"

"Whew, that was close! I'm okay; I'm okay," he said bravely as he checked himself over for cuts, scratches, and bruises.

"With all da clatter in there, I ain't so sure," Stranger said.

"Well, the broom nearly got me and that cat's claws nicked my tail but I was too fast for them. No problem. They didn't have a chance!" Pronto panted, "I used my secret weapon."

"Spits?"

"Yeah, spits."

"I think from now on we'll just listen from out here. It'll be safer for both of us," Stranger suggested, bending his ear toward a crack in the backdoor.

While the Weasel Warren Warlock experimented with conjuring spells on the raven by twitching his staff, he softly suggested to Evilla, "If you dip those things in that rancid potion nobody will buy them at the pumpkin sale." With a zap, the raven became a lizard.

"The smell is too sour even for my nose, my sweet."

"What do you mean, my darling? You have always loved my delicious stews," she replied.

Gulping hard he turned his head so she wouldn't see the grimace on his face then turning back wearing a fake smile. He noticed the disappointment on her face. "Yes, of course I do my love, but I also know that your favorite flower is the bitter smell of deadly nightshade and unfortunately, our human cousins do not have your sensitive nose for the finer things in life."

"Really?"

He rolled his eyes up trying not to offend her. "They prefer the smell of roses and homemade apple pie! Fresh-baked bread, lemons, and pine."

"How can they? Those smells make me gag. How could they not love the charming aroma of rat legs over a bed of stinging nettle and skunk cabbage with slug trail sauce?"

He turned and looked at her. "Sweetness," he said in a caring voice, "you'll catch more flies with honey than with vinegar. I think you'll have to add a sweet fragrance if you want the humans to buy the pumpkins."

With the flick of Dreadmore's wrist, the lizard turned into a rat.

"Rats!" he blurted. Frustrated, the warlock zapped the rat and turned it back into a rather dazed raven. "Humph! I'll get this right somehow," he claimed. "Now, how do I get this thing to turn into a gargoyle?"

This time the raven's eyes flew open wide and he began squawking in earnest protest.

"Hmm...yes, my darling, Dreadmore, I believe you have something there. Humans have such weak constitutions don't they?" Then to herself once more, she mumbled, "Now what do I have that would...?"

She hunted through several drawers and hutches then suddenly remembered. "Ah ha! I've got it!" she said, snapping her fingers. "Now where would she be?" In a flurry, she rummaged through various cupboards, boxes, and chests with even more vigor. "Hmmm, not here either. Now where did I put her...? She must be here somewhere. I know she's here."

All eyes watched as she stormed the rest of the cottage. Finally, the wizard suggested, "What about your special place?"

"My special place? Yes! That's it! The cellar!" The gasps from all those who had ever experienced the cellar sucked up air in the room.

"Not the cellar!" gulped several weasels in unison, pressing their quivering bodies against the cottage wall. They all knew what was in store for anyone sent down into the cellar.

The witch once again reached for the set of keys attached to the shiny silver chain around her neck, unlocked the door latch, a padlock at the top of the door, another at the bottom then pulled back the deadbolt. She pulled with all her might on the handle until the rusty hinges creaked in protest and the decrepit door begrudgingly gave way.

A whining creak echoed throughout the cottage while the chill, musty air rushed up from the deeps, filling the room with the odor of mold and damp.

She struck a match to light a lantern at the top of the stairs leading down into pitch darkness and a throng of bats roared out of the cavernous hole and swirled madly around the room. The panicked weasels ducked and covered their heads as the bats circled in a black mass and then, as suddenly as they came in, flew up and out through the chimney into the skies of the dark night.

"Fly my beauties," the witch cackled. "Fly!" She peered into the darkness as her eyes adjusted to the dim glow from the lantern flame. "It has been awhile since I've been down there. Hmmm, now let me see."

Not wanting to upset her arachnid friends who scrambled into dark hide-a-ways against the intrusion of light, Evilla crept slowly down the creaking stairs, gently brushing away the thick cobwebs so as to not destroy their sticky traps. As she descended deeper, empty chains with metal manacles appeared, hanging on the damp stone walls. Rats, spiders, beetles, and bugs scattered across the stone floor, fleeing the approaching torchlight.

"Now where did I put that...?"

A whimpering voice came from the darkness. "Please your great witchness, please let us go."

"We promise to be evil. We really will," sobbed another.

The approaching glow from the lantern illuminated two dirty, ragged, scrawny weasels hanging helplessly from manacles at the bottom of the stairs.

"What? Who's there?" the witch answered in surprise.

"Just us your witchness?" the frail voices replied in unison.

"Just who?"

"Treasel and Veasel."

"Oh, you two. I completely forgot about you two." She turned toward the source of the wimpy voices.

"We promise to be bad, really bad. We won't be good no more, your witchness. Pu-leeease, we beg you let us go. We've learned our lesson, pu-leeeese," they promised, squinting and cowering in the lantern light with the witch towering over them.

"You had better!" she snarled, unlocking their chains. "I should leave the pair of you urchins down here for another week or two. Or for that matter, I could let you rot down here forever!"

"We promise..."

"Oh, be quiet, you weeping, glorified rats!" she yelled. "It just so happens I do need all the slaves, er, workers I can get."

"Oh, thank you, thank you, thank you, your evilness!"

She reached for another key around her neck and unlocked the leg shackles. "Now get up stairs and help with the pumpkins! Make sure you set a good example for the others to work even harder!"

"Yes, yes, your evilness, we will, we will!" They scurried up the stairs as fast as they could before she changed her mind.

"Now, where was I? Oh, yes, now where is that little...?" She pulled open more dust-laden cupboards, rearranged shelves, and pulled open drawers of the old broken-down furniture lying around.

Under a pile of scrolls on a dusty shelf, she found a small wooden cupboard. "Ah ha! Now I'm getting warmer. I knew you were here somewhere."

Once again she reached for her neck and grasped the set of keys that hung on the silver chain. "Here it is," she whispered, selecting a tiny key to unlock a miniature door. She reached inside and pulled out what looked to be a miniscule tarnished birdcage, covered in cobwebs. Holding it up to her lantern, she gazed at the delicate figure inside. "There you are my pretty," she sneered at the struggling shape pulling at the bars. "I knew you'd come in handy some time or another."

When the witch emerged from the cellar, Mordred's ears pricked up and his green eyes focused with great interest on the tiny being buzzing inside the cage.

"What is that your evilness?" asked Sleazel.

"This, my little oaf, is the Sugarplum Fairy."

Outside, Stranger gasped. "Dat's where she is. Quacks wondered why she ain't been around the farm lately. He'll want to know about dis for sure."

Pronto ran up Stranger's nose and put his tiny arms over his mouth to hush the raccoon. He had no desire to be discovered again.

Inside the shack, the witch opened the cage and reached in. "Yeow! Why you little..." She grabbed the fairy by the wings and pinched until Sugarplum had no choice but to come out. "You bit me! I should throw you into my pot for that little stunt!" She snapped, licking her wounded finger.

Mordred licked his lips and swatted at the fairy as she dangled before his eyes.

"That might make it just a little too sweet, my Dearest," the warlock warned Evilla as he zapped the raven again turning him into a dazed grizzly bear. "You know how fussy humans can be. Too sweet, too salty, too hot, too cold, too spicy or too bland—they're never satisfied."

"Yes, perhaps you're right."

The grizzly stood to its full size on its hind legs and roared. The grumpy bear turned one way then the other as the swarm scattered and he swiped at the scurrying, squealing menagerie of fur but the terrified weasels had squeezed out of every crevice and crack they could find. Before the angry grizzly could attack his wife, Dreadmore pointed his wand and transformed the bear into a rabbit. Smelling the change, the remaining weasels promptly turned and hissed at the potential prey. As the weasel pack circled, Dreadmore twitched the want again. Anything but a rabbit, he thought, and the rabbit became a wolf.

The weasels scattered again as the bewildered wolf was zapped into a beagle.

"Get back in here!" the witch boomed to the other weasels who had scrambled out the door.

Much to Stranger's shock, Beazel, in his attempt to escape, had run and opened the window above where he and Pronto hovered in the shadows. The light from the cottage nearly caught them as they plastered their bodies against the wall. Luckily, Diesel had yanked Beazel back inside before their presence became known.

"Whew, that was close!" Pronto squealed.

"Wha, wha, what's dat smell?" Stranger blurted when the odor from within the cottage wafted out and reached their noses. It was the first time he had smelled the witches brew.

"Now you know what I went through!"

"Sufferin' catfish, how can anyone stand dat?"

"Yumpin' Yimminey, pay attention, pay attention," Pronto squealed, returning to put his ears back at the door.

Back in the cottage, Evilla shook Sugarplum's frail body over the cauldron and watched the sugar cascade from her. "Maybe this will tame your savagery, you glorified little flying imp!"

When she was satisfied she had enough sugar, she threw Sugarplum back in her cage, slammed the door, and locked it. Instead of taking her back downstairs into the cellar, she put the fairy into another darkened cupboard and locked it with yet another key from the chain around her neck.

"I'll deal with you later," she said, rubbing her finger again. "You horrible, nasty little scoundrel! Perhaps I'll let Mordred play with you as a reward!"

Pleasantly surprised, Mordred licked his lips in anticipation.

Within seconds the brew's colour had changed from dark purple into a clear sugar-like glaze and smelled like sweet plums.

"That's much better," Dreadmore mused as he turned the beagle into a toad.

"Okay, now let's get started," the witch commanded. "Sleazel! Get your boys to move that chair closer to the pot, and bring the stool next to it. That's right, now use my spell books to form a set of stairs."

The weasels obeyed.

"You three," she ordered a group of weasels frozen in shock. "Help Meazel on the other side and get that chest over here. Diesel, give them a hand."

The weasels rearranged the furniture so that there was now a rather odd looking stairway on either side of the cauldron. The witch extended her boney fingers toward some weasels standing at the doorway. "You! Good for nothings. Bring my beauties in!" she demanded.

In no time, the weasels formed into a long line and began carrying the orange globes up the makeshift stairs. One after another they reached the boiling pot where the witch dunked each pumpkin into her magic potion. Once they dripped in her sugary ooze, the weasels carried them out the back door and back toward the pumpkin patch.

"Heh, heh, heh, what a surprise our human friends are going to have on Halloween!" she rolled her eyes in delight.

"I cannot wait," the warlock responded.

She cackled in high-pitched joy and started to hum her favourite tune in pure delight. The warlock hummed along with her. "I'm the Weasel Warren Warlock and I'm coming after you. Boo!"

As the procession made its way out the back door, Pronto, having left a few scattered Sunflower seeds, took off like a bullet and ran up a drain pipe while Stranger scurried, just in time, to hide behind an old rain barrel. Being as quiet and as still as he could in the shadows, he could near his own heart pounding in his chest. As each weasel passed, he could hear their grunts and groans as they struggling with the heavy pumpkins. Stranger could have reached out and touched them. They were so near he could see and smell their panting rancid breath exhaling into the fall air. They didn't see him nor did they have time as they struggled to push and drag the pumpkins back to the patch.

Inside, one of the weasel minions bobbled a pumpkin at the caldron and the witch quickly yelped. "Be careful, you fools. I do not want to spill one drop of my wonderful elixir."

The weasel struggled frantically with the scruffy Veazel and Treasel to rebalance the teetering ball.

Lowering her voice, the witch continued, "There is none to waste. I must save a few drops of my precious brew."

"Yes, my sweet, we will need more for our other friends," the smiling warlock added, winking at Evilla.

"Shhhhh, you fool. No one is supposed to know about that!" she chided and went back to dunking the pumpkins carefully and delicately, one at a time.

"I believe, my dear, nothing can stop us now."

"We can't be too careful, my sweet."

Throughout the long night, the weasel rabble marched like a finely tuned military machine. The production line labored back and forth to the Pumpkin Patch until all of the pumpkins had been collected, coated with the sugar glaze and carefully put back in place.

And it all happened under the watchful eyes of Stranger, Pronto and, of course, Patches.

Bruce Kilby

# Chapter 8

# What to Do

The following morning started on McSimmons farm just like every other morning. Blissfully unaware of what had happened the night before, the rooster crowed right on time at dawn, the sparrows started to sing along with the irritating craw of the Stellar's Jay, and Sneezer scared the crows away exactly on time as Farmer McSimmons burst out of his front door with his shotgun.

After things had settle down again, Mr. McSimmons set about doing the routine chores like cleaning out the barn, while Mrs. McSimmons milked the cows then collected a basket full of the hens' eggs for a nice breakfast at six. To the McSimmons' it was just another brisk fall day. All seemed perfectly normal.

The animals, on the other hand, were in quite the tizzy.

The sun had risen by the time Stranger and Pronto had made it back to the farm. They made a beeline to Quack's nest amongst the reeds.

"What do you mean, 'they dunked the pumpkins into a potion'? Who dunked the pumpkins?" Quacks demanded, rubbing his eyes and scratching his left hindquarter.

"Da weasels."

"The witch," added a full-cheeked Pronto.

"I know the weasels, but why?" Quacks inquired with patiently.

"Dunno," the two spies replied.

"Okay, okay, you'd better fill me in from the start."

"We was doing as you said, Quacks," Stranger began again. "We hid under Patches' coat and waited for da weasels to show up. Dat's when I met an old buddy from da city."

"Yeah, Punk the Skunk," Pronto interjected with a nod.

"Excuse me? What does this have to do with...?"

"He was hiding. He was sent out on da same bus as me. He's a skunk who's tryin' to make his way back to da big city. He might show up here. I said he could come here for a couple of days to rest up."

"A skunk?"

"Yeah, yeah, a white one with a black stripe. You can't miss him."

"Why would we want a skunk around he...? Wait a minute! A white skunk with a black stripe? Why is he white?"

"We was in dis warehouse see, 'n he was always joking around. One night he was trying to do what the da rats do and he climbs a cable. But when we heard da sirens comin' he panicked and he fell into a vat of chemicals."

"Then what?" Quacks tilted his head in confusion.

"When we finally dragged him out his fur had changed colour. His black fur went white and his strip went black. I dunno what was in dat vat but it was potent."

"I see."

"He's a leader of dat crazy Italian gang ya see in da papers. Da Stinkerolas, or somethin' like dat. We call him Punk the Skunk but he's harmless. He's an old friend of mine."

"Okay, okay, I get it, but what about the weasels? Did you see any weasels?"

"Sure enough, just as you suspected, in they came back when the night was darkest. Me and Pronts, and oh yeah, dat Duke too, were watchin' out for 'em. When dey started walkin' off with da pumpkins we followed them, just like you said to."

Pronto nodded then pantomimed his actions of running back and forth, hiding under or behind various imaginary hiding spaces and brushed his brow when he was almost seen by Beazel.

Stranger interrupted him. "All the way back to the witch's house."

"Witch's house!"

"Yup. Da witch's house. She was hootin' and hollerin' so loud she was scarin' da beweezes out of dem weasels."

"This changes things for sure," Quacks agreed. "What did she say?"

"Well, Pronto got in and climbed up to the rafters to see what was goin' on and to listen."

Pronto went into another speedy pantomime, talking fast and re-enacting how the witch created her potion, holding his nose and fainting to show how the witch's brew got to him. When he described how he Sleazel and the rest of the weasels discovered him he tore around the nest site, leaping to nearby branches while mimicking the weasels chasing him. When he came to the part when he was almost caught by Mordred and sprayed him with his spits, more sunflower seeds exploded from his cheeks as he imitated the broom trying to swat him and finally, squeezing out the crack in the wood shutter.

Quacks shook his head. "I didn't understand one thing he just said."

"I kinda guessed that. As I said, we got back to da witches house. Pronto was hiding in da rafters and I was listenin' by da back door. The witch was mad at da weasels for takin' so long. She threw stuff into her potion boiling in da pot. Something about monsters feet and tongues! Phew! It stank real bad."

Pronto held his throat gagged, turning in a dizzy circle before flopping to the ground.

"Da witch loved it but da warlock said it should be sweetened so humans would like it. Oh yeah! You'll like dis part. I just remembered. The witch pulled out der Sugarplum Fairy from a cage to do it!"

"Sugarplum! So that's how she disappeared. We have missed our old friend for a long time. The apples, cherries, and especially the strawberries have never been as good since our little one disappeared. What did the witch do with Sugarplum?"

"She grabbed her by the wings and was going to throw her in the pot! Sugarplum bit her. That witch was so mad!"

"Whaaaat?" Quacks' eyes widened.

"No, no, she didn't throw Sugarplum in! Da warlock stopped her. Da witch shook her over her brew. Sugarplum couldn't stop her and she dumped a lot of sugar into da stinky concoction to make it sweet and smell nice."

"Then what?"

"Then da warlock changed a raven into a Grizzly bear! Then he changed it into a rabbit. Da weasels liked the rabbit. Den he changed da rabbit into a wolf and everybody went crazy again. Dats when we nearly got caught again."

By now, Quacks was totally confused. "Then what happened?"

"He changed it into a beagle."

"No, no! What about the pumpkins?"

"Oh yeah, one by one dey dunked the pumpkins. We nearly got caught when da weasels brought them out the back door!" Pronto began to re-enact the scramble but Quacks held up a hoof.

"Thank-you. That won't be necessary," Quacks said. "Then what?"

"All night dey went back and forth, back and forth until dey had glazed every pumpkin in da Pumpkin Patch!"

"Why does she want to put a spell on the pumpkins?" Quacks wondered out loud.

"Dunno."

"Listen, well done, the pair of you. You both deserve a treat. I saw Mrs. McSimmons crying earlier which means she spilt some milk today so if you go to the back of the barn you can help yourselves. There's a hole in one of the grain bags. Just don't get caught. I'm gonna need your help to get to the bottom of this."

"Tanks boss," Stranger said, turning to go.

"Wait a minute," Quacks said, stopping the pair just before they disappeared into the reeds. "Tell everyone I'm calling a special Farm Council meeting tonight. This is really important. Everyone has to be there. If there are any complaints, tell them we have to prepare for the petting zoo."

That evening, the barn was in an uproar. The one time of year all the farm animals on McSimmons farm dreaded was the infernal annual petting zoo at the pumpkin sale. Only Angus the bull didn't care; he knew no one would dare come near a bull with horns. To ensure he wasn't bothered, he also snorted and stamped his feet at anyone who approached, and charged, or at least pretended to, whenever anyone came near. He loved to watch terrified humans scrambling over the fence and running for their lives. His trick worked because Farmer McSimmons wouldn't allow children to play anywhere near an aggressive bull in the petting zoo!

Every year Farmer McSimmons set up the petting zoo at the pumpkin harvest to encourage children to understand and respect farm animals. That was the idea anyway. Some children, however, had different ideas.

Folks of Weasel Warren and nearby Badgerville came to pick out their Halloween pumpkins for carving and making pumpkin pies. They chatted with Mrs. McSimmons, drank hot chocolate and hot apple cider, and ate roasted chestnuts while the children were let loose in the petting zoo.

"They scare the...wits out of me!" clucked Henrietta. "All those human young'uns chasing me and my sisters around the pen all day! I just don't know. I wish I could fly like other birds," she said, flapping her short wings. "We never get to rest the whole time they're here. Listen here! Do you know I can never lay eggs for at least three days after this horrible affair!"

"I lost three tail feathers last year!" Mildred protested.

"I always have my tail pulled at least a dozen times," complained Barley, the donkey, not wanting to be left out.

Mary Lou, the ewe, slowly shook her head. "I feel so sorry for my cute lambs getting hugged and mauled by the little 'uns wanting a new pet. Don't they realize my lambs want to stay with their Mama and not go home wagging their tails behind them with human children?"

"They try to ride me!" Penny the pig said indignantly. "All day long I'm running away from those, those ... hooligans! I must lose ten pounds in one day!"

"Not that she couldn't do with twenty!" Molly mumbled under her breath.

"What did you say?"

"They like to hear you squeal," said Angus with a chuckle. He didn't care one little bit what the others would have to face all day Saturday.

"That's enough!" ordered Quacks. "We have a very serious situation here!"

"Yes, I'd say, this is the most stressful time of year for us hens," Henrietta piped.

"And the geese," said a voice from the back.

"And the ducks," quacked another.

"I understand your concern, Henrietta, and all you others who have to face the petting zoo Saturday," Quacks said, lowering his voice, "but we also have something strange going on at the Pumpkin Patch."

"What?" Everyone in the crowd gasped.

"What could be more dreaded than petting zoo day?" cried Daisy.

"Evilla, the witch!" said Stranger.

A sudden intake of air could be heard as fear gripped the whole council. No one spoke as the shock set in. Then the chatter started all at once.

"She's back," Quacks stated.

"Not again!" spat Molly in disgust.

"I saw Mrs. McSimmons looking for her broom the other day. I wonder..." Sneezer muttered.

Daisy interrupted. "I heard she turned Gerome the Gnome into stone! Or was that the warlock?"

"That was years ago! What about Patches? I hear he can't move!" Mildred cried.

"A freeze spell is what I heard," answered Penny.

"Did he say freezing? I'm not cold. I find it quite warm in here," said Barley, by now totally lost.

"What did he say?" Henrietta clucked. "Who is that lone stranger anyway?"

"You have to listen to Stranger," Quacks said as he brought his guest forward. "Now don't get all concerned," he added, knowing the ducks and hens would worry about having another egg stealer in the mix. They ignored Quacks and began nervously clucking and quacking, twitching their tail feathers, and prancing in circles.

"Now calm down, calm down. This is Stranger. He's from the big city!"

"And what did he do in the big city?" sneered Molly.

"Well, I admit, he was on the wrong side of the tracks. He got caught up in an egg-snatching round up by the pound and got relocated. He's on some new identity program big cities have."

"Egg snatcher! From the big city! Get a rope!" shouted Mildred.

"I know, he had a rough past," injected Quacks "but he's put that past behind him. He has been here working for me, and the council, for the last few months. He's our prowler."

"Prowler! Have you been spying on us, Mr. Quacks?" Daisy harped indignantly.

"Tsk, tsk, typical politician! Don't think just because you wear that hat you can do anything you want! No, sir!"

"No, no, no. I brought him on when we had the coyote problem a few months back. Remember Henrietta? That mangy coyote was after your chicks, and you, Mildred, the ducks and geese were going crazy over all the tricks he pulled trying to get at their ducklings and goslings. Well, Stranger got rid of him for you."

The din subsided. "All of a sudden it was peaceful around here again. We haven't seen him around anymore. Whatever happened to mangy cur anyway? Did he get relocated?" Mildred asked.

"You could say dat," Stranger said with a devilish grin. Pronto nodded his head vigorously.

Quacks clanged Daisy's bell. "Listen up folks. Let's get on with it. You know the Skysquawkers in the Northwoods..."

"Who wouldn't? Those noisy things! Squawk, squawk, squawk! That's all they do!" complained Mildred the Mallard.

"And take our grain!" moaned Daisy the cow.

"And my apples!" groaned Molly the horse.

"Settle down. Remember Duke Skysquawker? Well, he saw something."

Murmurs and complaints could still be heard from the onlookers in the public gallery, which was the hayloft or the empty stall next to the water trough.

"When Duke Skysquawker and Sneezer came to me last night, they told me that there was something strange going on at the Pumpkin Patch. Duke had seen pumpkins disappearing from the patch. He thought the weasels were stealing them but when they saw Duke, they dropped the pumpkins and scattered back into the woods."

A ripple of murmurs crisscrossed the barn. "So I sent Duke, Stranger, and his faithful friend, Pronto, to check it out and keep an eye on it. They too saw something very disturbing."

"Tell us, what you saw Stranger?" asked Molly.

Quacks stepped down and turned the milk crate platform over to Stranger. While Pronto acted out the details, Stranger spoke. "Well, we was up at da patch, watchin' over it when, sometime after midnight, da weasels came back to steal da pumpkins."

"Oh my," gasped Mary Lou and Sue the Ewe together.

"Dere was too many to stop 'em so we just followed 'em. Just like da Boss, er, I mean Quacks here, asked us to. Me and Pronts followed them deep into da forest until they came to a clearing at da old woodcutter's house."

"Ooooh," said the crowd from the gallery.

"The old shack is pretty run down now but inside da Witch of Weasel Warren and da Warlock were preparin' some kind of stinky potion in her black pot."

Pronto mimed the stench by holding his nose, spinning around, and flopping on the ground as if dead.

He now had everyone's complete attention. One could have heard a spider spin a web.

"Pronts stuck his nose inside to see what went on but nearly got caught by da weasels and da witch's cat." Pronto continued to mime out the chase using his best sneak and prowl imitations, with much more bravado than the actual scared little mouse he had been a few hours earlier.

"Den the warlock changed a raven into a bear. A grizzly bear!"

A huge gasp came from the assembly followed by the usual chatter and another round of nervous clucking.

"Okay, okay, quiet down everybody. He changed it into a dog," interrupted Quacks, purposely leaving out the change to a wolf. "Let's get back to the story."

The gathering slowly calmed down and refocused on Stranger.

"Anyway, we heard Evilla dunk each pumpkin with this brew that was sweetened by the captive sugarplum fairy."

Another gasp went through the crowd. "The Sugarplum Fairy? Our friend, Sugarplum? Awww!" said Daisy.

"I loved getting my apples and carrots sweetened with a little sugar on them. I think we need to do something, don't you Barley?" said Molly.

"Huh? Wha...,"

"Oh never mind. You liked them too, right?"

"What were we talking about?"

"Sugarplum!"

"Oh? I thought he was talking about pumpkins."

"What did she do with Sugarplum?" asked Silly Willy the Billy goat.

"They keep her locked up in a cage somewhere," Stranger explained.

"Oh!" cried the disbelieving crowd.

"What did they do with the pumpkins?" asked Sneezer.

"All the pumpkins were taken back to the patch covered with this magic glaze."

"That's odd," said Penny. "Why would they want to do that?"

"My question exactly," Quacks replied.

"Maybe she just wanted them sweeter for all the children. You know Halloween is the favourite day for witches," said the innocent Mary Lou, the ewe.

"Nah, I don't trust her, I don't trust her one bit," said Henrietta. "And them weasels! You can't trust them as far as you can throw 'em!"

"Where did she get so many weasels?" asked Penny the pig.

"Yeah, how come so many?" asked Billy.

"Dunno," replied Stranger.

"Well, I'm ready for WAR!" Angus bellowed.

"I agree with Angus," Barley brayed.

"Yeah, she weren't in no happy, happy mood when we overheard her," Stranger continued. "She wanted to throw sugarplum right into da pot but da warlock stopped her."

"That's it! War it is!" bawled Angus, pawing the floor with his hoof.

"Not so fast. Wouldn't that be the last resort? Some of us could get hurt," said Penny. "Maybe we could negotiate or something."

Angus groaned and rolled his eyes. "I don't think so!"

A lot of chatter rose from the group as each one translated to the others what Stranger had said. None of the gathered animals had understood Pronto's mime.

"Okay, the question is, what do we do now?" Quacks posed.

Do we go to war or not?" Angus demanded over the incessant babble. "Has anyone got any better ideas? It's getting late."

"Well, perhaps our stranger friend might want to prowl around the witch's house and keep an eye on her," Mary Lou piped up, managing to ignore Angus.

"Yes, try and see what she is up to and maybe look for a way to get Sugarplum out of there." Pondered this for a few seconds.

"Save Sugarplum!" several of the others shouted.

"Perhaps we could all keep our eyes peeled on the Pumpkin sale on Saturday," added Daisy.

"We'll see what we can do but me and Pronts will keep an eye on da witch," Stranger said huskily. "And da Warlock, too."

"Don't forget the weasels," clucked Henrietta.

"Duke and I will watch the pumpkin sale seeing we're not in the petting zoo," Sneezer offered. Another huge groan rose form all those who knew they were doomed for the weekend madness.

"Okay everybody, we all have our jobs to do," said Quacks. "Good luck. Let's get a good night's sleep."

"What's wrong with going to war?" Angus moaned as they all left the barn. He looked at Barley. "A good charge into the valley of death makes you feel alive! I love a good charge, don't you?"

"What?"

"Some of us might even be prepared to die for such a good cause, don't you think?"

Barley rolled his eyes and stopped listening.

Bruce Kilby

Bruce Kilby

# Chapter 9

## The Petting Zoo

It was a crisp but clear morning with the sun shining through the auburn and rust coloured leaves of the sweet chestnut trees. Many of the trees' spiky seed balls had fallen and broken open on the ground. Farmer McSimmons loved the taste of sweet chestnuts and would roast them at Christmastime over a crackling fire in an old 45-gallon drum. They were so good he had regular customers who came to buy them and sing a few Christmas Carols every year. Today though, Mrs. McSimmons was serving roasted peanuts, hot cider or marshmallow chocolate for all the folks who came out to buy pumpkins.

Saturday morning had come all too soon for the McSimmons' farm animals, especially those that were selected for the dreaded petting zoo. The goats, lambs, pigs, had all been ushered reluctantly into the makeshift corral near the barn, except for Quacks who always managed to hide in the reeds. Barley the donkey, Molly the horse, nervous Henrietta with her entourage of other hens and chicks, several geese, Mary Lou the ewe with her newborn lambs and Silly Willy the Billy goat had to participate. Straw had been laid out on the ground and hay bales circled the pen for seats. The only good thing for the animals was the fresh hay and feed McSimmons had put out for them to munch on. Several buckets of carrots and apples sat waiting for guests to treat their favourite animals. All was arranged and ready for the crowds to show up for a special day at the McSimmons' petting zoo and to buy their Halloween pumpkins.

Not only was McSimmons all set but so were Duke and Sneezer. Duke was watching from the top of the barn trying to disguise himself as the weather vane and keeping as still as he could so as not to be seen, not that anyone would have noticed anyway. He had a good view of the surrounding area and especially the road leading to the farm.

Hoping not to be noticed by any playful children, Sneezer strategically hid under the red and white-checkered tablecloth that displayed the apple, blackberry, and pumpkin pies Mrs. McSimmons had lovingly made and would be trying to sell to bring in a little extra income. He too lay as still as he could but unlike Duke, he knew he was in considerable jeopardy of being noticed. Small children had the knack of running around in and under small places and discovering…trouble. The last thing Sneezer wanted was for his long ears or tail to be pulled by inquisitive and out of control kids.

Slowly at first, the Weasel Warren town folk began to arrive. There were always those who came extra early to beat the crowd and get the "perfect" pumpkin. Other farmers like to chat without town folk interrupting but they had to get back to the chores on their own farms.

First one or two, then many cars arrived. Two or three children bounced out of the back seats and race off to the hot chocolate and apple cider stand. After gulping down their drinks, they would head to the petting zoo for a hair-raising chase until their parents, corralled them and dragged them off in search of the perfect pumpkin.

After trudging the field, they came back with their selected treasure.

Some folks took two or three when they noticed the shimmering aura and sparkly coating. In the sunlight, each pumpkin glistened and wore a blue-white coat as if covered by a heavy frost. As the morning went on many more of the nearby Badgerville folks and outlying areas arrived.

"How did you get your prize pumpkins to sparkle?" asked one neighbour.

"What are you feeding these pumpkins?" asked another. "They look so sweet and tasty."

"Well, I really don't know," said Farmer McSimmons, studying them for the first time. "We haven't done anything different from other years and we haven't had our first frost this year so I really cannot explain it." Holding one up into the sunlight, he remarked, "They do look rather good this year, I must admit. Well, all the better for you as there's no extra charge!" he replied with a smile.

The petting zoo went exactly as expected, or unexpected depending on which side of the fence you were looking from. The animals were chased, hugged, petted, and grabbed to the squeals of the children and the animals. Penny, panting heavily, had made several laps of the pen to get away from a young boy who tried to ride her, thankfully, without much success. Others were luckier. Molly and Barley were given way too many carrots and apples as well as nice scratches on their snouts. Farmer McSimmons had to stop two boys from trying to climb up on Daisy. They had hoped to ride the cow like a cowboy in a rodeo. Silly Willy the Billy goat rammed two teasing boys who chased the chickens but the boys just laughed and thought it was all a game. By noon, kids were running everywhere creating an excited din of squeals and giggles.

Mrs. McSimmons was so pleased that all of her pumpkin pies as well as most of the others had been bought, including her roasted peanuts. Everyone was enjoying the marshmallow hot chocolate and sweet cider.

It was Duke who saw them approaching first. A strange antique-looking metal beast drove up the long driveway toward the farm. This vehicle was different from the usual pickup trucks and sedans that the locals drove. This smelly, eye-glowing, metal beast was nothing like Duke was used to. All black with big rounded fenders and blacked out windows, it had a long room at the back with eerie curtains hanging in the rear windows. It might have once been a fancy car but today was old, rusty, and carried an unmistakable pall of gloom.

Sneezer's hackles went up. He sensed danger but didn't know what it was. Both animals could sense spookiness but could not see it. To Duke it had the smell of death and to Sneezer, an unseen evil intension. Neither liked it one bit. Sneezer growled and tried to sniff but instead began to sneeze. He slapped a paw over his nose so as not to be detected by any wondering child.

The animals in the pens could sense the evil presence and shied away, twitching nervously.

Out of the beast's belly came a sinister-looking couple, like other humans except for green aura surrounding them. With pale skin, un-kissed by the sun, and eyes that glittered with evil, they wore long black coats and hats that hid their faces from all who dared look.

The woman strolled up to Mrs. McSimmons' pumpkin table. "Oh, what nice pumpkins you have," the woman cackled before her voice altered into a pleasant titter.

"Why, thank you," said Mrs. McSimmons, backing away. "Would you like to buy one?"

"No, no, we are just checking. Are they selling?"

"Why yes, they are going just like hot cakes. Everybody likes the sparkle they have this year."

"Good, good, just as I plan...er, I mean, hoped for you and Mr. McSimmons." She changed the subject. "Nice pies you have there."

"Thank you. They are fresh apple pies just out of the oven. I picked the apples from the orchard myself. There is also blackberry but I have run out of the pumpkin. Would you like to buy one?" she said, staring at the pale green aura.

"No, no, way too sweet for me. We are into more, shall I say, organic stews, aren't we, darling?"

"Yes, my sweet. A rodent or two with poison ivy mixed with gravy and potatoes is one of my favourite stews. Especially when seasoned with dried fire worms!" He closed his eyes and licked his lips dreamily.

"Ow! What was that for!" the mystery man said rubbing his side from the quick jab he had received from his companion's sharp elbow.

"May I have some of your hot cider?" the dark lady asked, ignoring him.

"Why, yes, of course." Mrs. McSimmons started to pour them each a cup. "You're not from around here are you?" she asked trying to see under their low-brimmed hats.

"No, my dear, we have just returned to the area a little while ago and have a nice little home in the nearby Northwoods." The strange woman turned her head away as if to hide her face.

Sneezer could no longer hold back. He poked his head out from under the table with a deep guttural growl.

Duke, also sensing their aura of cruelty, swooped down from his perch on top of the barn and buzzed at the heads of the couple like he would if chasing a hawk trying to steal eggs.

"Caw, caw, caw!"

"Well, I never! Unfriendly little…animals aren't they?" the woman said, taking a swipe at Duke.

"Oh, I am so sorry, it is very unlike them," Mrs. McSimmons said with a tiny smile on her lips. "I don't know what got into the pair of them."

"I think we've seen what we've come to see and had better be on our way," the woman in black snorted. "Don't you think so, darling?"

"As you wish my sweet." In a huff, they both turned to leave.

That's when Duke noticed a strange amulet hanging around the man's neck. As the couple strode past Gerome the Gnome standing at his solitary post by the wishing well in the front garden, the amulet began to glow. "Caw, strange, strange, caw, caw," he said but only Sneezer understood him.

The odious couple got into their long metal beast and roared out of the farm, kicking stones back toward the astonished crowd.

As the couple left, Mr. McSimmons came and stood beside his wife. "Strange couple, those two. I don't think I've ever seen them around these parts before."

"They gave me the willies. They upset Sneezer and all the other animals. Even a crow attacked them."

"How odd, the animals seemed okay with the other folks who dropped by. What did they want?"

"I don't know. All they asked was whether the pumpkins were selling."

"Why would they come all the way here just to ask if the pumpkins were selling?"

"And they didn't even buy anything!" she replied, rather ruffled by the whole incident.

"They must be from the city," McSimmons answered. "That would explain it."

The Northwoods had always looked a lot different in the daylight. Brighter, cheerier; birds sang. In stark contrast, the cottage looked unnatural—dark and dank with evil clinging to every corner.

Stranger and Pronto had found their way back to the cottage in the early morning without being detected by the weasels. They saw the strange couple dressed quite differently from the night before and watched them depart in a peculiar metal machine. As they drove away, the familiar voice of Evilla bellowed out from the curtained window of the black beast. "Keep a close watch on this place or I'll have your hides!"

"Yes, yes, yes, madam wickedness! Of course we will," Sleazel replied, bowing. No sooner had she left, the weasels went back to playing their favourite game, flicking hazelnuts toward the well wall. The one who came the closest would win a trout caught from the river as his reward.

From behind a rock in the bushes, Stranger and Pronto were patiently watching.

"Good she and dat warlock is gone. Now dat she is, we need to get inside da house," Stranger whispered.

Pronto protested, pointing to the weasels and acting out getting caught and playing dead.

"Yeah, I know, there's too many of them to fight off but don't worry. We won't take 'em straight on. We just hafta wait for da right opportunity." He lifted a paw into the air to make sure he was downwind. He didn't want to be detected by the whole pack of weasels should the breeze change direction.

When a cheer went up from a winner, Stranger and Pronto decided to move in closer. They sneaked to the side of the cottage and scurried along the front porch. Pronto squeezed through the crack in the door, climbed up a chair and onto the window ledge to unlatch the window, hanging on the handle until the window opened. Stranger, using his nimble front paws, pried it open wide enough for him to slip in through the gap.

"Take a look around, Pronts but don't make a sound see. We don't want any trouble with dose guys," Stranger whispered, glancing over his shoulder at the weasels below. They had got in unnoticed by those outside but neither of them had noticed the shadow that was moving stealthily across a dark corner of the cottage.

Pronto scurried across the floor, up the side of a buffet and hutch and investigated various bowls and cups. Stranger jumped up onto the warlock's desk next to the raven, which was indeed still a raven, chained to the perch. After checking a few books, scrolls, and strange vials holding various animal parts, he moved on to another cupboard. As he sniffed behind a bowl, he heard a faint squeak. Standing on his haunches, he put his ear up close to the cupboard's keyhole.

"Help me, help me," came a familiar voice.

"Hey, I've heard dat voice before. You, you are da...,"

"Sugarplum Fairy," she replied.

"Yeah, dat's it, da Sugarplum Fairy. You're da one that bit da witch's finger." He chuckled at the thought.

"Yes, I really don't like doing things like that but I was, well, desperate."

"Looked good to me."

"Can you get me out of here? Please?"

"The cupboard is locked. Do you know where she kept da key?"

A big sigh came from within the cupboard, "She always kept her keys on a chain around her neck."

"Around her neck?"

"Oh dear, I guess I'm never getting out of here."

"Don't worry 'bout dat Miss. We'll get you outta dere somehow. We raccoons are pretty good with our front paws. We can get into anything. There ain't been a garbage can made that I can't get into!" he said, trying to cheer her up.

Sugarplum sighed.

"Pronts, look around and see if we can find something to pry the door open." Stranger cast about for anything that could jimmy the lock. "Knives? No too big, a pair of scissors? No, too awkward, hmmm."

Just as Stranger reached to open the drawer in the night table, Mordred pounced, landing right in front of the startled raccoon. Mordred growled and hissed in Stranger's face in a vain attempt to scare the intruders away.

Now, Stranger was a city raccoon, so he wasn't fazed one bit. He had faced many an alley cat in his day, most a lot tougher and meaner than any pampered house cat in the country. Stranger hissed back, much louder, fiercer, and more frightening than anything Mordred could have ever mustered. "You don't wanna take me on, cat? I'll punch you so hard and so fast you'll think you're surrounded!"

Mordred reached out his paw to take a swipe at Stranger who leapt back just in time.

"Okay, buddy, that's enough from you," Stranger warned, leaping to his feet. "Choose your window. You're leaving!" He sprang at the cat, swatting Mordred's head three times. Smack, smack, smack. The cat's head snapped sharply left, then right, then left again as each swat struck. "Dere's more where dat came from," Stranger hissed.

Mordred's bravado suddenly left him. With one whimper, he disappeared under the bed to lick his wounds.

Pronto continued to scoot around the cottage checking into every nook and cranny that might hold a key or for anything that might pry a lock. He passed the entrance to the cellar and looked down into the black hole for a moment but thought better of going there. If he had to face that mystery, he would do it with Stranger but he was not going down there by himself. Avoiding the cage of rats, he searched in pots, boxes, crates, jars, bins, and tins. He found needles and pins and a paper clip but no key.

The raven didn't make a sound as he walked back and forth on his perch as far as the chain would allow. His eyes seemed to plead for help. His only blessing was that the Warlock had not left him as a toad, a snake, or a slug.

With great difficulty, Pronto tugged on the cap of a strangely ornate jug. When the lid finally popped open, a bizarre yellow powder puffed out into his face. With one whiff, Pronto's eyes crossed and he spun around, dazed and bewildered. He staggered and swayed dangerously close to the edge of the table. Before he could teeter off the edge Stranger kicked a cork stopper at the staggering mouse. The cork soared through the air and just as Pronto was about to plunge over the edge, the cork hit him squarely in the belly.

"Oooof!" The air gushed out of Pronto and he was sent staggering backward on to the table where he tripped over a spoon handle and landed in a bowl of Wart of Toad seasoning salt.

A little stunned, Pronto shook off the effect of the powder. "Holy hot tamale! That was close. Thank you Stranger, thank you," he squeaked.

"No problem, little buddy," Stranger said as he climbed the makeshift stairs and checked out the empty cauldron hanging over an unlit fire.

Pronto squeezed out from under the stopper and brushed off the salt, then licked his paw. "Eeeyuk, that's awful! Who could eat this stuff?" Before anyone could answer, he spotted something glimmering from behind a larger soup bowl containing wiggling leeches. He crept closer, sniffing, and making sure it wasn't a trap. There, hiding behind the bowl, he noticed the links of a silver necklace. Curiously, he pulled on the chain. It loosened but his little body was too small to free it completely. He dangled it over the edge of the shelf and jumped on the loop he had created in the chain. With all his weight on it, the chain slipped out and there, attached to the other end, was a set of old and oddly shaped keys.

"Lookit, lookit," Pronto gushed as he clung on to the chain with both front paws. "She musta left them behind!'

"Good job, Pronts!" Stranger said, he scurrying to the shelf. "She musta taken them off when dey changed into those get ups!"

Being much bigger, Stranger easily picked up the keys and carried them over to the locked cupboard. It didn't take long for Stranger to unlock the cupboard with his agile paws. Inside, Sugarplum sat, locked in her tiny cage. In no time, Sugarplum was free.

"Thank you, thank you, thank you!" she cried. "Those evil people have kept me locked up in that cage for a very long, long time." She stretched her arms and fluttered her tiny wings.

"No problem Miss. Didn't wants to see ya stuck in dere any longer. I know what it's like being caged, if ya know what I mean." He rubbed his nose with his sleeve. "We was sent here by Quacks and da Farm Council to get you outta here and find out what's going on with da pumpkins from da pumpkin patch."

"Thank you, my brave heroes," she whispered, kissing each of them on the cheek.

"Do you know why da witch put a spell on da pumpkins?" Stranger asked.

Before Sugarplum could answer, Snap! Pronto's tail had accidently flicked into a mousetrap behind a mason jar.

"Yeeeeow!" Pronto screamed.

Mordred's muffled giggle could be heard coming from under the bed.

"Stuff it, cat!" Stranger barked. The snickering stopped.

Stranger pressed his paw over Pronto's mouth to hush him but it was too late. Outside, he heard Sleazel shush the other weasels. Stranger knew it wouldn't be long until they decided to investigate.

"We've gotta go!" Stranger yelled snatching Pronto up in his arms. "Out the back!" he ordered.

"Wait a second," Sugarplum cried. "I need my wand! I have to have my wand!"

"Sugarplum, we have no time!" Frantic, she looked back into the cupboard. Seeing nothing, she buzzed from shelf to shelf. Her wand could be anywhere. For all she knew, the witch could have destroyed it but she had to look. If she ever wanted to use her magic, she had to find it.

From the ledge by the window, Stranger could see that by now the weasels were halfway across the yard and starting to spread out. "Who's in there?" Sleazel ordered.

"Come on, Sugarplum, we have to go!"

"One more moment, I cannot get back to Fairyland without my wand; I have to have my wand."

"We have to go," Stranger pleaded as he watched the weasels getting closer and closer.

Finally, she saw a row of silver thimbles on the top shelf of the dish cabinet. One appeared strangely different from the others because from under it, she saw a familiar golden glow streaming out like sunrays.

"There it is!" she declared lifting the thimble to reveal her wand.

"Gotta go, nooow!" The weasels had almost reached the door.

"I said, 'who's in there?' Is that you cat!" Sleazel's voice demanded even louder now.

"I'll delay them!" Sugarplum answered and in an instant dashed away and flew through the crack in the front door.

"Noooooooo!" Stranger yelled but it was too late. She flew under the door and buzzed straight toward the gang of gnarly weasels. Bravely, she flew in front of Sleazel's eyes and defiantly hit him on the nose with her wand to make sure he noticed her. As Sleazel swatted at her, she took off in the opposite direction away from the cottage.

"Get her! Get her!" Sleazel demanded pointing toward the sparkling creature streaking away as fast as it could go. The tower of weasels whose paws were on the door handle of the cottage, jumped down off of each other, wheeled, and scurried after the buzzing fairy. "Her witchness will skin us alive if she escapes! We have to get that fairy!" Sleazel screamed.

To make sure they followed her, Sugarplum flew low and slowly to entice the weasels to jump and claw after her. As they did, she bobbed up and sped out of the way. For her, this was fun again and it felt wonderful using her wings once more after being cramped in the tiny cage for so long.

"Wheeeeeee!" she giggled as she dodged in and out, back and forth, wild and free once again.

The confused weasels yelped, gnashed their teeth and leapt this way and that, into and around each other but never once coming close to capturing the fast fairy. Without realizing it, Sugarplum slowly drew the hoards of weasels deeper into the woods.

Under the watchful eye of the raven, Stranger and Pronto slipped out the back window unseen by the weasels and scurried off into cover of the woods.

Mordred breathed a sigh of relief but remained hidden under the bed, unwilling to come out until he knew the coast was clear.

RAT-B-GONE

Bruce Kilby

# Chapter 10

## Gerome the Gnome

"What happened to you!" a startled Quacks said when the two prowlers came back through the reeds to his pad.

"We got out just in time," Stranger said out of breath. He had been carrying Pronto but now put him down. "We were checkin' out da witches place as you said to," he puffed. "We freed Sugarplum," he wheezed, "but Pronts got his tail snapped in a mouse trap!" Stranger held his sides as his panting slowed.

Turning around, Pronto showed Quacks the painful and unwanted accessory. The mousetrap still held his tail in its steely grip.

"Da weasels heard da noise and came a-runnin'. Sugarplum diverted dem away while we slipped out da back." His panting had begun slowing down. "I ran all da way back. No one saw us. I'm sure of dat."

"Well, that's good news. At least Sugarplum is free but what do you mean 'diverted them away'?"

"We got in da house undetected and had a look around. Found Sugarplum locked in a cupboard. It took us a while to find da keys. We had a little trouble with da house cat but I sorted him out, if ya know whad I mean."

"Yes, yes, go on."

"Well, we found da keys da witch left lyin' around see, and got her out of da cage," he said. Pronto protested. He had been the one to find the keys.

"Yes," Quacks said, acknowledging Pronto, "but did she know about why the witch wants the pumpkins?"

"She was about to tell us when Pronts here got his tail caught in da trap and da weasels started comin'."

Pronto once again showed his painful appendage and pleaded for the trap to be removed but his appeals went unnoticed.

"Okay, then what?"

"She went to distract 'em," Stranger continued.

"I hope she got away? We've missed her a lot around here."

"Not sure. I tried to stop her but she wouldn't listen." Stranger rolled his eyes. "Last I saw, she had a whole bunch of angry weasels chasin' her but it looked like she was havin' an awful lotta fun doin' it." Rubbing a paw across his chin he asked, "You've known Sugarplum a long time?"

"Oh yes, a very long time. She's a good friend of ours. She sweetens up all the apples, cherries, carrots, and other stuff at harvest time."

"What would da witch want with her?"

"Witches and fairies have been enemies for eons. Good versus evil, you know. She came here some time back to try and free her cousin, Gerome the Gnome. She thought a witch or warlock had something to do with his capture. Then suddenly she disappeared. We hadn't seen her since."

"Does anyone know how to release a mouse trap?" Pronto squeaked as loudly as he could, while cradling his throbbing and swollen tail and grasping the menacing wooden contraption attached to it.

Just then, Duke and Sneezer broke through the reeds. Both still appeared visibly upset about the strange visitors to the farm.

"Wow, you two look like you were in the petting zoo!" Quacks declared. "Sit down before you fall down."

"Caw, caw, we saw evil, we saw evil. Caw, caw, caw!" Duke squawked noisily, flapping his wings.

"Yup," said Sneezer. "They creeped me out too. This weird looking couple came to the pumpkin sale. I could sense evil all around them. All the animals in the zoo did, too. They didn't like 'em one bit. Henrietta and her chicks ran away to the far side of the pen; Molly got skittish and started to rear up and Penny squealed like she was being attacked! Most distressing!"

"Does anyone know how to release a mouse trap?" Pronto's squeaky voice could barely be heard above the babble.

"Who is this weird couple and why were they there? Did they buy any pumpkins?" Quacks asked.

"Don't know who they were. They wore black long coats and big hats and their skin looked funny. Scary dudes. They only asked Mrs. McSimmons how the sales were going. Didn't buy nothing. They came in a long metal beast that smelled like death."

"Many deaths, many deaths, caw, caw," Duke added.

"I growled at them and I'd have taken a chunk out of them if I could! But the smell, oh, that smell of wickedness, made me sneeze a record fifteen times in a row! I nearly got caught by the kids!"

"You said a metal beast that smelled like death. I think we know who they were," Stranger commented.

"Yeah, yeah, the witch and the warlock, the witch and the warlock!"

Pronto declared. “Now can someone get me out of this thing?”

“It was da witch and da warlock,” Stranger interpreted. “We saw ‘em leave da woodsman’s old cottage in dat eerie looking metal beast. Horrible, it was. All dressed in black. That’s how we knew da coast was clear to go have a look inside.”

“What about the weasels?”

“Da weasels guarding da place were a piece of cheese.”

“A piece of cheese?” Quacks queried.

“Ya, you know boss, I mean, Quacks. Easy cheesy.”

“Oh, I get it.”

“That’s it!” Pronto’s set off at top speed and circled the nest in a blur, ensuring that his tail and the mousetrap slapped each face on his way around.

“Hey, what was that for? Wait a minute…is that a mousetrap he’s got on his tail?” asked Sneezer, peering at Pronto.

“Caw, caw looks like a mousetrap to me, trap, trap, trap to me, caw.”

“Oh, I’m sorry, little buddy. I completely forgot about da trap.” Stranger nestled his annoyed little friend between his paws. “Does anyone know how to get this off of him?”

“Careful, careful,” Quacks cautioned as Duke held down the trap with his paws and Stranger pulled at the clamp.

After several attempts, Stranger sighed. “It’s no use Pronts. I haven’t got da strength.”

“What’s that noise?” Sneezer had nothing wrong with his hearing and was first to notice a familiar but somehow different buzzing sound.

“Sounds like a dragonfly to me,” Quacks offered, familiar with the sound from around the pond.

"No, this is a little different. It sounds like..." said Mildred paddling toward the nest.

"It's me!" Sugarplum exclaimed as she swooped up hovering above them.

"Sugarplum! It sure is nice to see you again!" Quacks smiled broadly, surprising all the others. "We have all missed you very, very much. The fruit has never been as sweet as when you are around."

"Thank you, it is so nice to be back. After we escaped, it took me a while before I could shake off those nasty weasels but at last…I'm freeeeeee!" she sang out as she pirouetted in mid-air. "Thanks to these two brave heroes," she said, smiling down on Stranger and Pronto. Then she saw Pronto's dilemma. "Why, what do we have here? Oh my goodness, are you still stuck in that awful thing, my dear?"

"Do you think you could help me Buddy?" Stranger begged. "We can't get it off him."

Pronto nodded feverishly, a look of despair on his face.

"I do think I can help. There's nothing I would rather do than to help the friends who helped saved me!" Sugarplum waved her little wand and with a tinkle of bells, turned the trap into sparkling sugar. "Now, little one, go dip your tail into the water and the trap will simply dissolve!"

But before Pronto could move, Quacks said, "Hey, wait a minute. I'm never one to miss a sweet treat!"

"Me either," Sneezer agreed, giving the sugary trap a lick. "It's been a long time since I was allowed sugar."

"Ya don't have to ask me twice," added Stranger, breaking off a corner and popping it in his mouth.

"Caw, caw, sweet, sweet, caw."

In the surge of tongues that followed, Pronto received several friendly face washes but in no time, the trap had dissolved leaving Pronto rubbing his sore tail while the others licked their sticky lips.

"Dat was goooooooood!" Stranger said with a sigh.

"Soooo, here we are." Quacks brought everyone's attention back to the question at hand. "We still don't know why the witch coated the pumpkins with her potion."

"Oh, I know," said Sugarplum. "I heard everything that went on from under the floorboards when I was locked in that cage in the cellar."

"Oh good! What is that evil woman up to?" asked Quacks. "It can't be anything good, I'm sure."

"You're right, Quacks. She wants to make Halloween wicked. Bring back all the real ghouls and ghosts."

An audible gasp came from the group even though Sneezer had no idea what a ghoul or a ghost was. "What's Halloween?"

"Shhhh," Quacks hushed.

"Ogres and orcs," Sugarplum went on.

"No, not ogres and orcs!" Quacks cried.

"Vampires and werewolves, and of course, all the real witches and warlocks!"

"I think I'll go back to my comfy doghouse," Sneezer announced, his tail between his legs.

"She wants humans to fear the night again and children to hide under their beds! She wants to reclaim the All Hallows' Eve by releasing all the hideous evil creatures of the night!"

"That's not good," Quacks declared, shaking his head. "Not good at all."

"Caw, caw, not good, no, not good, caw, caw," echoed Duke.

"I'm definitely going back to the doghouse," Sneezer muttered.

"Shush, shush, what about the pumpkins? Why do you think she put a potion unto the pumpkins?" Quacks wanted to know.

"I never heard why she put a potion on them or what she plans to do with them. I only know its part of the plan."

"Well, it's more than we knew before," Quacks said. "Thank you, Sugarplum." Quacks looked around to the others. "What do you all think she's up to?"

Sneezer answered first. "I'm just a guard dog. I was quite happy being a guard dog. All I have to do is bark at the crows. Every morning, bark at the crows. Simple. I think I need a nap back at the dog house."

"I never knew witches, warlocks, fairies, or gnomes ever existed before today. Let alone witch's spells or, or, potions! Dunno what she's up to," Stranger growled. "By da way, what's an orc?"

"Caw, caw, I'm scared of Patches. Patches scary," Duke replied.

Stranger stared at Duke. "Well, he ain't no use." Turning to Quacks, he went on, "I've seen a few creeps in the back alleys before but dese guys, I ain't had da pleasure. They may be scary but not to me. I'll take 'em on. I sorted out dat cat, didn't I? I'll sort these two out, too!" Beside him, Pronto bravely boxed the air with his tiny fists.

"I think we are gonna need more than just our fists, friends," Quacks replied.

"Gerome the Gnome might know," Sugarplum suggested.

"What? All the gnomes I knew of were turned into stone years and years ago," said Quacks.

"Not all gnomes were but yes, Gerome was changed by a magic spell, stolen by the wizard or witch many years ago. He would still know more magic than I do. In our world, they are the craftsmen of good magic, potions, and spells. And Gerome, the statue in your front yard, was a master."

"What is she talking about? What gnomes?" asked Sneezer. "Gerome has been sitting in the front yard ever since I can remember. Mrs. McSimmons goes out and paints him now and then."

"Yes, humans tend to do that. How embarrassing for Gerome! He won't like this at all," she giggled. "You'll see many of my cousins painted in bright colours like the seven dwarves."

"Nice," said Sneezer.

"No, no. Humans think they make the garden look pretty but gnomes are not supposed to be seen. Ever! They are garden elves who help Mother Nature do all kinds of wonderful things but they are still elves."

"Oh!" a collective gasp of understanding rippled around the circle.

"Elves know much magic! For centuries they did their work under the cover of shadows to hide from prying human eyes. They are not meant to be displayed like a clown for every animal to sniff and…well, you know."

Everyone turned to look at Sneezer who, realizing what Sugarplum was saying, felt a pang of guilt.

"They would just shudder if they were to see themselves displayed like that. That's why I was sent here, to see if I could free them so they can help Mother Nature again. I have searched for years, all over the world, to find out which witch or wizard stole the magic. The only ones left that I know of are the two evil characters who captured me. It had to be them! The Weasel Warren Warlock has changed many of my cousins into stone in gardens all over the world. It's an epidemic!"

"I'm so sorry," Sneezer said admitting his remorse at what he has been doing to Gerome. "I didn't realize. Is there anything we can do?"

"I don't know. The witch caught me several years ago through a simple mistake. Every night when he had his bath, the warlock took an amulet from around his neck. It looked the right size and the right colour so one summer night, I sneaked in through the window to try and find it. I needed to see if it was what I was looking for. Unfortunately for me, just before I could grab it, her giant pet spider dropped down from the ceiling, nearly scaring me to death. When I backed up from fright, I got caught in the hairy beast's web. I must have squealed because before I knew it, she was behind me and bam, I was in her cage!"

"On no!" Stranger whispered.

"Grab what?" asked Quacks.

"King Oberon's amulet. He had it made for his wife Queen Titania to turn evil gargoyles into stone. It was meant to be used only on the evil beasts from below, never on elves or gnomes."

"Oh, no," the listeners all said at once.

"They used it for evil. Not only gnomes were changed but forest creatures such as deer, bunnies and squirrels, as well."

"Yeah, I've seen dem around. I think humans gather them up and put dem in dere gardens!" Stranger added. "Maybe they are part of da plan?"

"No, I don't think so. Humans have long forgotten about elves, gnomes, and fairies. They think of us as fairytales and legends. Cute things for the imagination but not real," Sugarplum replied.

"And dey think dey are so smart," Stranger huffed.

"In my search, I have seen horses, elephants, and even mermaids turned into statues. I was sent by Oberon, the King of the Fairies, to get it back and try to stop all this wickedness."

"The warlock still wears the amulet around his neck, I am sure of it. I think we saw it today at the farm," Sneezer said.

"Caw, caw, blue glow, blue glow. Caw, caw."

"Yeah, Duke's right! I saw it start to glow blue when he passed Gerome in the garden today," Sneezer added.

"I knew I was right. I just knew it! It was the Weasel Warren Warlock! We have to get it back," she replied.

"How can we get at it with him always wearing it and with a pack of weasels on guard outside?" asked Quacks

"And the witch," said Sugarplum. "Don't forget the witch. She put me in a cage but I'm not sure what she'd do to the rest of you. She only keeps what is useful to her."

Sneezer gulped. "It's time for a nap," he said and started to leave.

"No, no, we need everybody we can get," Quacks said. "Let's put our heads together and we should be able to come up with something."

"How can I bark at the crows if she turns me to stone?"

"Caw, weasels, weasels!"

"Yeah, and them weasels. They can be vicious."

"I have an idea," Stranger replied. "We use distraction. We used to pull dis off to avoid dose sons of human animal catchers in da big city." Noticing the stares he added, "Er, I mean da authorities."

They all huddled closer to hear his whispered plan.

Bruce Kilby

Bruce Kilby

# Chapter 11

## Oberon's Amulet

Stranger, Pronto, Sneezer, Sugarplum, and Quacks waited in the bulrushes until the first glow of dawn. They planned to sneak up on the weasels while everyone was asleep. When the first splinter of gold appeared in the sky, they crept through the woods on tiptoes, quiet as ninja warriors. Duke circled overhead while the others crept up to the clearing around the woodcutter's cottage.

They peered through the bushes expecting to see a weasel sentry or two with the rest of them asleep around the well, porch, and outbuildings. But there was not one weasel to be seen.

"Dat's strange. Dey were all here last night," Stranger whispered.

"I see a lot of bunnies though," said Quacks.

"Look at them all," said Sugarplum

"It's not Easter is it?" Sneezer added.

"I see dem too," said Stranger. "I wonder if dis is a rabbit trap?"

"I don't think so," said Quacks, looking around. "There are no lights on in the cottage. It looks peaceful to me."

"Too quiet for my liking. I've seen traps like dis before," replied the ever-suspicious Stranger.

Even Duke couldn't see anything from his hiding spot in the trees above.

"Deir faces do look very familiar." Several of the rabbits had the same markings as the weasels.

"I think the weasels are now bunnies," said Sugarplum. "I knew the witch would not have been happy when she found out I had escaped."

"Do you think this was their reward?" Quacks asked.

Stranger shrugged. "Well dat part of the plan is out da window."

"We've still got to get in there or get them out," said Quacks.

"Looks like we need Plan B," said Sneezer.

"Yup," said Stranger. "Er, what Plan B?"

"You don't have a plan B?" Sugarplum looked from face to face.

"Well the way I see it," Stranger began, puffing out his chest, "half our job is done. If we make enough noise, da bunnies will scatter and da warlock will come out to find out what's going on. Den Duke can do his stuff."

"Duke 'do his stuff'?" asked Quacks.

"You know, dey like shiny things. I've seen 'em fly down and take brooches right off ladies hats. Humans think dey are being attacked but really, all dey want is da shiny thing."

"Well, I'll be," said Quacks looking up at Duke who bobbed up and down, shrugging his shoulders.

"Ya, some friends of mine told me dat when dey raid crow's nests for eggs…er, not me of course, dey's seen da nests full of jewelry, coins, spoons, anything dat glitters."

Duke hopped up to a higher limb and looked away.

"Mrs. McSimmons wondered where some of her jewelry went," Sneezer explained, "and Mr. McSimmons lost his pocket watch just last month."

"Dere's no time for dis," said Stranger. "Deal with him later. We must all be ready to pounce."

"We certainly will." Quacks gave Duke a stern look. He put one hoof up to his eyes then pointed to Duke's then back to his own. Duke knew that meant Quacks would be keeping a close eye on him. "Okay, let's get on with it."

They broke out of their hiding place and spread out to surround the cottage from three sides. One familiar looking rabbit started to squeal the alarm but its whimper could hardly be heard, especially by anyone in the cottage.

Once they were in place, Stranger gave the order. "Okay, Sneezer. Time to let her rip."

Sneezer started to howl, sending rabbits scattering for their lives. Duke squawked in the tree while Sneezer bayed as loudly as he could.

"Howooooooooo! Howoooooooo!"

Meanwhile, Sugarplum squeezed under the front door to find the witch and warlock peacefully snoring in their big bed. The raven fortunately, was still a raven and slept quietly chained to his perch. Mordred was nowhere to be seen.

With the first rays of light coming through the small window, Sugarplum flew over the dimly lit room to the resting souls. Even with the howling outside, the rhythm of their snoring didn't change. As if in concert, one snorted in air while the other wheezed noisily through fluttering lips.

Sugarplum jabbed the warlock's nose with the point of her wand. The warlock flung a hand up as if swatting a fly, missing Sugarplum by only a breath. Just as she was about to poke him again, she heard a whiny growl behind her. Mordred stared intently at the fluttering wings in front of him.

"Now you wouldn't want to hurt me, would you?" she said innocently.

The cat fixated on the movement of fairy wings flitting back and forth, licked his lips and growled once more. His tail flicked back and forth. Thinking quickly, she waived her wand over him and sprinkled magic sugar dust all over him. "There, that should do it."

Doused in sugar, the cat's mood changed instantly. A sweet smile curved on his mouth and he lay down at the foot of the bed and started to purr. He licked his lips then began cleaning himself from head to tail. The magic sugar was so irresistible he forgot all about Sugarplum.

Switching back and forth from the witch to the warlock she kept poking and they kept swatting. Finally, one large blood veined eye opened just as Sugarplum stabbed her once more.

"YOU! Why I..." the witch yelled, sitting up and thrashing at the dodging fairy.

"What's all the fuss about my darling," the warlock's groggy voice asked. "Whose dog is that, howling outside?"

"Dog! What dog? I'm looking at this, this beast buzzing in front of me. Come here, you little imp!" She leapt out of bed, swatting harder.

Zipping this way and that, Sugarplum guided them to the front door while evading each grab and swipe. The warlock, annoyed by the noises outside, had still not noticed Sugarplum's distractions and grabbed a broom. He swung open the front door and stepped outside, ready to deal with all the howling and squawking.

"Now!" Stranger yelled then sank his sharp teeth into the warlock's ankle.

"Yeeeeeow! What the...?" the warlock howled in pain, staggering sideways.

He tried to swat the broom at the raccoon clutching his ankle. With a mighty leap, Sneezer chomped down on the wrist that held the broom. "Yeow!" the warlock cried again, shaking his arm to dislodge the dog.

Pronto ran into the cottage and straight up the witch's nightdress.

"Eeeeeeeeeeek!" she screamed, her arms and legs jerking wildly as she tried to whack Sugarplum and the strange thing running around inside her dress.

"Mordred, do something!" she yelled. Contented, the cat just lay there licking his paws. "Why you lazy, good for nothing…wait till I get…" She squirmed and squealed, "this thing..." slapping at her own body, "out!"

At the precise, right moment, Duke started his dive. "Caw, Caw," he squawked as he streaked down. Tilting his wings at the right angle, he swooped in and grabbed the amulet with his claws, snapping it from the warlock's neck.

Quacks scrambled into position and tucked his rotund body behind the warlock's knees. Sneezer jumped up and planted his big front paws on his chest. The warlock staggered backward.

Sploosh! The surprised warlock plunged into the rain barrel with only his head and feet poking out from its top.

"Ruuuuuuuuuuun!" Quacks yelled.

Pronto and Sugarplum shot away from the witch, Duke soared up into the sky, while Stranger, Quacks, and Sneezer ran as fast as they could across the yard and back into the woods.

"Whaaaat! Where's my staff, where's my wand, get, get me out of this..." the warlock screamed and splashed. "You will suffer for this! I will get the lot of you!"

Once safely away, Stranger looked back and through the trees saw the crack of blue lightning flash followed by hearing the witch's screeching voice yelling, "Get them you oafs!"

Looks to me like dey're weasels again! he thought.

Being the slowest and definitely the most out of shape, Quacks, the pig, was out of breath and soon left behind by the others. He was desperately trying to catch up but it did not take long before the weasels were hot on his trail and closing in. Quacks could see them to his left and his right trying to get in front of him to cut him off from the rest.

Sleazel was determined not to fail the witch again. "Get him, boys! We'll have roast little porky tonight!"

Quacks, gasping for air, thought if he could make it to the far end of the pond, he'd be safe. All those painful and embarrassing swimming lessons Mildred had taught him just might save his life. He ran as fast as his heart would let him. "If only I can get to the pond!" he gasped.

He wasn't sure if weasels could swim but if they could it would be very hard for them to attack. Unfortunately, the weasels were almost upon him and biting at his heels. His heart sank when he realized, I'm not gonna make this!

With less than a hundred yards to go, the weasels had indeed caught up to him. Diezel jumped on Quacks' back while Meazel grabbed his ear and hung on. Others ran between his legs trying to trip him. With little grace, Quacks was hauled down, tumbling over and over and finally skidding to a halt. With the taste of victory at hand the weasels were about to pounce.

It was Sleazel who saw him first and started to back pedal immediately. Others put the brakes on when they saw Sneezer standing there with hackles up, teeth bared in a vicious snarl and growling with a deep guttural snarl. Stranger was standing beside him and although smaller, the weasels were well aware of how vicious a raccoon could be when cornered.

Sneezer grabbed Diezel in his jaws and threw him into the bushes. Stranger snapped at Meazel making him let go of Quacks' ear.

"Get out of here while you can. We'll handle this." Sneezer said to Quacks, snapping at several weasels.

"But what about you?" Quacks squealed.

"Don't worry about us. Now git!" Stranger commanded.

Weakened, Quacks knew he couldn't fight the weasels off. He also knew Sneezer and Stranger couldn't either, at least not for long. He ran down the path toward the orchard sounding the alarm. "The weasels are coming! The weasels are coming!"

With the Sneezer's element of surprise now gone, the weasels started to gain confidence. Now their own hackles rose up and baring their teeth, they stealthily circled their prey. They surrounded the two brave warriors now standing back to back ready for the attack. For a few moments it was like a Mexican standoff, growling, snarling, and hissing at each other. No one wanting to make the first move.

Circling, Teazel, Greazel, and Beazel took the left side while Sleazel, Meazel, and Diezel took the right. Fearing most the jaws and large teeth of Sneezer, they turned their attention toward Stranger but to get to him they knew they had to go through Sneezer.

"Get them!" Sleazel ordered in a raspy hiss and lunged first. He went for Stranger and the others followed. Meazel and Diezel went for the tail while Sleazel went for the neck but Stanger, who had been in many an alley fight, viciously tossed them off with ease. Teazel, Greazel, and Beazel and others focused on Sneezer but his height gave him the advantage. He grabbed two in his teeth and kicked two others at the same time with his hind paws.

The melee was a blur of fur, gnashing of teeth, yelps, and snarls. Weasels flew in all directions as Sneezer and Stranger ferociously defended themselves but Sneezer was no longer in his prime and it didn't take long before he began to tire. When he looked down at Stranger bravely fighting off the unrelenting attackers, he found new energy and lit into them again. He knew they couldn't hold out much longer as each nip from the weasels weakened them a little more each time.

Attack after attack kept coming and each time, Stranger and Sneezer scattered them again. One jumped on Stranger's back and went for his neck but Sneezer spun around and swiped the rodent off with his front paw sending him rolling into the bushes. At the same time Stranger ran through Sneezer's legs to nip at another weasel trying to attack Sneezer's back legs. Three more jumped onto Sneezer's back tearing at his security sweater while others jumped clung to his jowls to bring him down. Sneezer cried in pain as five or six more gripped his front paws. With the weight of so many weasels he was slowly being forced into submission.

Stranger fought ferociously as he too was swarmed but being younger than Sneezer, he managed to fight many of them off. Slowly but surely he realized that the sheer number of attacking weasels would win this one.

"It's been good to know ya, Stranger!" Sneezer whined in pain.

"Come on buddy, you can do it!" he answered nipping at one of the weasels holding on to Sneezer.

"Now we've got them!" Sleazel shouted. "It's supper time!"

No one had noticed the dark cloud approach from the Northwoods until it was too late. The throng of ebony wings circled above them without a sound. With lightning speed, the next thing the weasels saw was the sight of hundreds of crows knifing through the sky toward them. With Duke in the lead, the black swirling mass attacked with extreme fury, pecking and clawing unmercifully.

The weasels put up a brave vicious defense against the ravenous attack, scratching, snapping, and snarling but to no avail. Crows are practiced scavengers and can use their beaks with needle like accuracy. From a young age they had been taught how to grab fur while in mid-flight. They never missed with their beaks or claws as they swooped from every direction. If a weasel fended off one bird, another attacked from behind, and another from the side. To the crows, this was as easy as picking cherries.

When the weasels could stand the onslaught no longer, the fight was over. They retreated hastily back into the forest for cover, yelping, scowling, and hissing as they went. The crows continued to swoop down taking pecks at them until every last weasel had disappeared into the underbrush. As quickly they had come, the crows disappeared into the sky leaving the forest, Stranger, and Sneezer in stunned silence.

"Run you cowards!" Stranger finally called out breaking the quiet. "Nuttin' like a good scrap to get the juices flowin' eh, Sneezer?"

"Well I..." he stuttered. "Wow, that was a close call. I don't think I could have lasted much longer." Sneezer was black and blue, feeling his age and unsteady on his feet.

"Yeah, but I think we had 'em!" Stranger interrupted with bravado while rubbing a nick in one ear and licking at the patch of missing fur in his striped tail. "We could 'ave finished 'em." Stranger said bravely with nicks and cuts all over him.

"I'm not so sure." Sneezer replied licking a bloodied paw." They were taking me down."

"Aaagh," Stranger dismissed. "One night in da big city, I had to fight off twice as many of dem wharf rats over some deep fried chicken bones! They were twice as big as dees guys and dat was in a dumpster!"

Before he could reply, Duke flew back alone and landed on Sneezer's back. "Caw, caw, weasels gone, weasels gone!"

"Ouch! Duke do you mind not sitting there, I am sore all over..."

"Caw, sorry, sorry, caw." He hopped to another spot.

"Or there, either."

Duke flew up to a nearby branch.

"Thank you, Duke, and all of your friends. You guys came in the nick of time," Sneezer wheezed, panting. "Looks like you saved me again, old friend. I'll never forget it."

"Caw, caw. Quacks sent us, Quacks sent us. Said you were in trouble, in trouble, caw, caw."

"Well, we couldn't leave da Boss now could we?" said Stranger.

Pronto dashed in a blur with his fists up, ready for action and concerned for his buddy.

"Good job you weren't here, Pronts. One of dem crows might have mistaken you for a weasel tail!"

Laughing more in pure relief than at the joke, the victorious crew leaned on each other and proudly limped back to Farmer McSimmons' farm. Duke flew off toward the rookery.

Bruce Kilby

Bruce Kilby

# Chapter 12

# Northwoods Roost

Back at the barn, Daisy gave Sneezer a wet sloppy cowlick to help soothe some of his wounds as he lay in a pile of hay. Penny applied a mudpack to Quacks' bites and scrapes while and anxious Mildred pranced in a circle primping Quacks' makeshift nest. Pronto gave Stranger the first aid once over, pointing out each scratch, nip, and missing patch of fur. Mary Lou the ewe pushed straw to pack some of the worst cuts. Molly had dipped a bucket into the water trough and was carefully pouring water to clean the cuts.

"We must look a sorry lot indeed," Quacks said.

"Ahh, it's nuttin'. At least we weren't dodgin' bullets!" Stranger replied.

"But without you two, I would never have made it. I would have been pork chops! I'm sure of it. I thought I was going to have to swim for safety and you know I'm not much of a swimmer."

A snicker rippled through the barn.

"They caught up to me so fast. I am so thankful to you both," Quacks said, ignoring the tittering.

"Who changed then back to weasels? It must have been the witch," said Sneezer.

"Warlock, warlock," Pronto hollered but his tiny voice fell on deaf ears.

"Yeah, dey run faster dan rabbits!" said Stranger

"We wouldn't have made it without Duke and his buddies," said Sneezer, "Thank you for sounding the alarm!"

"We gotta few licks in ourselves!" Stranger said proudly.

"Did you see where Sugarplum went to?" Quacks asked, now covered in bandages.

"Not since the witch's cottage," replied Stranger licking a paw. "Did anyone see her escape?"

Pronto dashed in front of Quacks and nodded while miming how he had run up the witch's dress and Sugarplum attacked her nose then sped away when Duke grabbed the amulet.

Sugarplum had indeed escaped the swatting of the irritated witch. In her parting glance at the witch, she saw lightning bolts streaming from the crone's fingertips. The warlock had escaped his watery trap and gripped his magic staff as he filled the air with his bellowing.

She had flown straight to the crows' roost to await the return of Duke who had flown away ahead of her. By the time she had reached the Northwoods rookery, all of the crows had flown. Not a soul was present. She hadn't realized the flock had heard and answered Quacks' frantic plea for help. All she knew was that they were not there and given time would return at some point. She decided to wait. The amulet was very important to her and the fairy kingdom so waiting a few minutes longer wouldn't hurt. In her anxious state, every second felt like an eternity.

Sitting on the forest knoll, high in the Northwood trees, she could see all over the rural valley of Weasel Warren. The view was incredible and she realized why the crows nested here. It gave them great advantage to see any predator approach but just as importantly, they could see the food.

When the crops were ripe enough to eat, or when fresh garbage had been taken out, they would not miss it.

She was finally free and soon would be able to complete her mission for King Oberon and return Queen Titania's amulet to Fairyland. It had been a long time.

Looking around, she saw many nests, all dressed in glittering treasures. Pieces of tinfoil, shiny candy wrappers, broken mirrors, coins, and human and even elfin jewelry were strewn throughout all the nests. She remembered that crows prized things that glittered and often seized whatever caught their eyes, much to the dismay of unsuspecting victims.

"Which nest is Duke's?" she asked herself. There was no way to tell. She flitted from one nest to another, desperately trying to find the amulet but after a few moments began to feel that it might be rude to snoop. Not wanting to offend the entire roost, she decided to wait for the crows' return.

It wasn't long before she saw the dark cloud of flapping wings rise from the trees in the distance and make their way back toward her. As they approached, the black mass blotted the sky. When they realized someone was near their nests, they protested the presence of this stranger.

"Caw, caw, who is she, who is she?" one large black crow insisted on knowing.

"Caw, protect the nest, protect the nest," said another, just as loudly from a nearby branch.

In fact, the racket from the protest became so loud that Sugarplum had to cover her ears. The nearby branches began to strain from so many of them landing and surrounding her.

Although spring had long since passed and the crow chicks had fledged, young crows were still there. The adults were still protective of their young. Sugarplum could see she was indeed an intruder here and that the birds were not friendly to visitors.

Caw, friend, caw, friend," Duke interrupted, his head bobbing. "Friend, friend, friend!" Soon the commotion subsided with just the odd squawk from a remaining protester or two.

"I am the Sugarplum Fairy," she said to the amazement of everyone. They all stopped squawking and the silence was instant. They could understand her. "I can speak many of the earth world languages, including crow." Noticing tufts of fur in beaks and claws, she added, "I see you have been in a battle. By the look of it and given all the fur, I'd say... weasels?"

"Caw, caw, helping Quacks, helping, caw, caw."

"Skysquawkers of the Northwoods rookery, that was very brave of you," she said complimenting the flock. "I hope you are all safe and unhurt," she added, noticing that a few had lost a feather or two. "I am sorry to intrude but I am here for the Oberon amulet that Duke took from the Weasel Warren warlock."

Just the sound of the warlock's name started them all squawking again. Even the crows knew fear.

"Bad, bad, evil, evil," they squawked.

They also knew that one of their cousins, the Raven, had been captured and was being used for evil experiments in the old woodcutter's cottage. They had heard his pleas each night begging to be freed.

"Please, don't be afraid. I will never hurt you," she said as she hovered above them. "You see I am a fairy and I can only do good deeds. I help Mother Nature put a little sugar on things to make the world a little sweeter." With a flick of her wrist she waved her wand and each nest had a ripe juicy candy apple nestled within it. "I always say a little sugar always helps make the medicine go down."

"Caw, caw," said the birds in amazement. Some hopped over to their nest and promptly tasted the apple gift.

"I was sent here from the land of fairies by King Oberon, the King of the Fairies, to find Gerome the gnome and get back the magic amulet that turns living things into stone statues."

The birds listened intently. No one had ever spoken to them nicely before except the pig down at the farm.

"The warlock stole it years ago from Queen Titania when she was visiting this world changing evil gargoyles into stone and chasing ghosts back into graves. Over these many tears, the Warlock has used it to turn many of my elfin cousins, the garden gnomes into stone!"

Another great ruckus arose from the flock. All animals can sense the difference between good and evil.

"Will you please give me the amulet?" she asked Duke.

"Caw, caw, sure, sure, amulet, amulet."

Sugarplum followed Duke to his nest in another tree. From beneath his pile of booty he picked it out of the nest with his beak and flicked it toward her.

"Thank you, my friend. You are so kind. I will return it to its rightful owner." She smiled as the amulet shrank down to fairy size and she slipped it around her neck.

"Oh, and by the way, I see a lot of other treasures in your nest that I think belong to others."

"Caw, Caw, shiny, shiny."

"Yes, shiny, and very tempting to have but don't you think that they were special to their owners?"

Duke tilted his head from side to side trying to understand what Sugarplum was saying. Neither he nor any other crow had ever given a thought to others.

"Thank you for all you have done. You are a true friend of the fairies and I will be sure to tell the king." She cupped his head in her hands and kissed him on his forehead. "I must leave now. There is so much to do. Good-bye for now. I am sure we will see each other again." Then with a swirl of her wand, she drew a fairy door in mid-air and opened it. With a spray of sparkling sugar drifting behind her, she was gone.

Back at the farm, all of Farmer McSimmons' pumpkins and pies had been bought, the hot chocolate drunk, and to the relief of most, the petting zoo closed.

In the town of Weasel Warren, all was in an excited bustle making ready for a spooky Halloween. The eager children, with the helping hands of parents, carved grotesque faces with sharp teeth and scary eyes on the orange squashes. Cobwebs with ugly black spiders hung in doorways, orange lights replaced porch lights, front yards became imitation graveyards, and paper skeletons and flying witches flew in windows.

Mothers prepared candy apples, caramel popcorn, soft taffy, or filled bags of store-bought candy to pay the ransom the costumed nighttime tricksters would demand.

At the cottage, the Weasel Warren Warlock and the Witch were preparing as well—not bagging candy or carving pumpkins but instead having the weasels make strange wooden cages. And not just one or two, but a lot of them!

The warlock, as usual, hummed his favorite song. "Up the walls and down the halls, I'm the Weasel Warren Warlock and I'm coming after you!"

When evening fell and several evenings before All Hallows' Eve, they took flight on their brooms to survey the preparations the town folk had been making. Poking their noses in at windows, keyholes, and down chimneys, they wanted to make sure the unsuspecting folks had carved their pumpkins and everything was ready for the witch's surprise.

"Isn't it wonderful, darling?" the witch whispered gleefully.

"Yes, my sweet," the warlock answered with a devilish grin.

Catching sight of the dark duo in the moonlight, or through in their bedroom windows, the town's children screamed in fright. By the time Mommy or Daddy came in to check on them, the scary figures were gone.

Evilla and Dreadmore were very good at this game. They had played it for centuries. They loved nothing better than to watch children scream.

"I saw a witch flying on her broomstick, Mom!"

"Yes, honey," a mother would reply, well past believing in witches and warlocks. "I think someone is too excited for Halloween to come."

"No, Mom, she was right there! Looking at me through the window!"

"Well they're gone now," mother said closing the curtains. "It's past your bedtime so go back to sleep."

With a cuddle, a kiss on the forehead, and a re-tuck into bed, the world was right again.

Or so they thought…

Bruce Kilby

# Chapter 13

# Sugarplum Returns

Fairyland, in the netherworld of magic, could only be accessed through secret portals hidden throughout the earth world. Fanciful creatures seen on the earth world can suddenly seem to disappear because they used these portals to escape the prying eyes of children. Sometimes these creatures accessed them to escape capture by trophy hunters or those who want to cause harm.

For some special creatures, these portals allowed them to conveniently travel to another part of the earth world altogether. Unicorns, Easter bunnies, leprechauns and elves, including one dressed in red, could come and go as they pleased. Fairies, on the other hand, could use their magic wands to create one of these special doors anywhere they wished.

Once inside, the enchanted Fairyland was full of wonder. With the air fresh and clean, beautiful rainbows reached over the sky, waterfalls glistened under the sunshine and snow-topped mountains, glistening like marshmallows, touched the blue skies. Deer, rabbits, and all kinds of exotic birds abounded near streams, and all the wildflowers were dusted in a sprinkling of powdered sugar. Mystical creatures such as unicorns, griffins, and winged horses roamed and frolicked freely without fear. All who dwelled within the realm felt happy and safe.

Young elves and gnomes floated in the sky in walnut shells held aloft by the sycamore tree whirlybirds seeds. Fairies skated across the lake chasing dragonflies, making soft ripple patterns in the water by dipping their wings. Others flew up into the sky and merrily designed the puffy white clouds into all kinds of shapes. With giggles the joy-loving fairies made turtles, funny faces, fancy bows, swans, and even a cloud lion.

The Easter Bunny's chocolate eggs lay in clutches everywhere; some wrapped in brightly coloured foil, some just plain, in white, dark, or the children's favourite, milk chocolate. Some of her eggs were solid chocolate and some filled with creamy fillings, candies, and other surprises.

Honeybees attended the lollipop flowers, wildflowers, and daisies that grew everywhere. Candy canes, gumdrops, jujubes, and suckers decorated every tree as far as the eye could see. Some winter elves claimed it was even more wondrous than Santa Clause's Toyland!

Oberon's splendid castle lay under a steaming volcano thought to harbor a friendly dragon. Nestled at the foot of the tallest waterfall, swans glided across the surface the clear blue green lake. Secluded amongst the trees on a cliff side, giant toadstools and mushrooms formed the palace and its spires. The palace had to be large enough not only for fairies but also the much larger elves and gnomes. To the little people, everything appeared overly large. To the bigger people, everything appeared exceedingly small.

A glorious white drawbridge crossed the lake leading to the main gate of the heavily defended castle. Soldiers guarded the gate not from those who lived in Fairyland, but just in case any evil creatures managed to find a fairy door and break in.

Elfin cousins called leprechauns, wood elves, and gnomes lived in small houses in the Shamrock villages on one side of the bridge while fairies, which are a lot smaller, lived in their toadstool homes in the surrounding rural community on the other side of the bridge. Wood fairies dangled their wooden homes from the branches high in the trees of the enchanted forests.

As Sugarplum flitted through the villages some of the fairies recognized and called out to her with happy smiles. "Good to see you again, Sugarplum!" or "Welcome back, Sugarplum, We have missed you." Then they returned to making their mystical treasures.

Sugarplum wanted to stop and visit old fiends but she knew she had to tell the king her story right away. Even though she had been away for such a long time and knew her parents would be have been worried for her, there was just no time to waste.

"I must see the king first. I have to let him know about the evil witch's plans."

As she whizzed past the shops she saw energetic gnomes crafting magical potions and gems. Earth elves worked at their forges making rings and amulets while wood elves carved wands. Special elves knew that the favourite spell in the human world was the granting of three wishes but only the most experienced elf could make it. They were known as genies or jinns.

But today, the whole village was abuzz with the news of Sugarplum's return. She skimmed across the drawbridge and waved at the palace guards who allowed her to enter the gate of the castle. Taking the corners on one wing, she flew through the great halls, past the library and the flag room, and down the great hallway to the throne room.

"Welcome home, Sugarplum," boomed Oberon, King of the Fairies, as she greeted the host of courtiers.

She bowed and offered the amulet to the queen.

"Thank you, Sugarplum, for bringing back Queen Titania's amulet," the king said. "We are most grateful. I can only guess that you have quite the story to tell us."

She now had the attention of the full royal court. "Yes, I certainly do your majesty. With the help of my friends in the earth world we took the amulet back from a witch and warlock who are guarded by their weasels."

"Who are these scoundrels?" the king demanded.

"Do you mean my friends or the witch and warlock?"

"I mean the witch and warlock."

"Her name is Evilla and his is Dreadmore."

"I know of these two vermin. They were just minor magicians during the Great War but we never did catch them. They must have slipped our patrols. What have those two scoundrels been up to?"

"With Queen Titania's amulet they have turned not just Gerome but many gnomes of the world into stone!"

"Oh my!" exclaimed the queen.

"They have been busy. I wondered why we have not heard from Gerome for such a long time. We have had several missing gnome reports so I had tooth fairies, wood elves, and earth elves all look for you on their journeys but no one found you, Gerome, or any of the others."

"If it wasn't for my friends, I would have never escaped the tiny cage she had put me in and locked away in a cupboard."

"Where are these parasites now?"

"They live in the old woodcutter's cottage in the Northwoods outside of the village of Weasel Warren."

"We will have to give them special repayment for their dastardly deeds. Don't you think, my darling?" he said, turning to his beautiful wife, Queen Titania.

"A special repayment indeed, Your Majesty," she replied. "Changing gnomes to stone! How nasty! And I did not appreciate them ripping the amulet from around my neck."

"You mentioned friends in the earth world," the king said, turning to Sugarplum. "Who are these friends?"

"There is Quacks, the pig, Stranger, the raccoon, his friend Pronto, the field mouse, Sneezer, the bloodhound, and Duke Skysquawker, the crow."

The king blinked and shook his head. "Excuse me?"

"I know they sound like a strange bunch but they were trying to stop the witch and her plan to make Halloween evil again."

"I see."

"There was Quacks the pig, Stranger the…"

"Make Halloween evil again, you say? We will have to see about that. Now tell me about these friends."

"Most live at McSimmons farm in Weasel Warren. Duke, the crow lives in the Northwoods rookery. He saw the weasels stealing the pumpkins from the McSimmons' pumpkin patch. Somehow their guardian, Patches, the Scarecrow, couldn't move to protect them."

"Sounds like a freeze spell, Your Majesty," a gnome advisor whispered in the king's ear.

"Possibly. Please go on, Sugarplum."

"The witch put a potion on the pumpkins and put them back in the patch. No one knows why but then the pumpkins were all bought by the town folk of Weasel Warren and Badgerville."

"Indeed! They have something planned and I would say it is nothing nice. How did you escape from these rapscallions?"

"Quacks, the pig, the farm patriarch, sent Stranger and Pronto to rescue me then helped Sneezer and Duke to get the amulet back."

"I see. It sounds like a brave band of animals to go up against a witch and a warlock!" the king said.

"Yes, very brave indeed. I would think the weasels were quite vicious, too," added Queen Titania.

"Very vicious indeed, my queen. They chased us relentlessly but we were able to escape. They seem to be under the influence of the witch and are terrified of her and the warlock."

"I have heard of this Evilla and Dreadmore before in other lands and other times of the earth world. I believe they are responsible for turning gnomes into stone for a long, long time. Thanks to you, Sugarplum, they cannot hurt anymore gnomes."

"My pleasure, Your Majesty."

"I don't know what these two are up to in Weasel Warren but we have to put a stop that too," the king said.

"Your Majesty," the elfin prince Landore politely interrupted. "We have so many battles with evil at this time of year. I need all of my warriors to guard the gateways to the underworld and do not have enough defense forces to take on these two."

"That is rather elfish of you, don't you think? We will do whatever we can, Landore," the king replied with a frown, "even if I have to go myself."

"Yes, Your Majesty," Prince Landore said, looking at the floor.

"Our worldly farm friends have done a good job so far. Maybe they can help us just a little bit more."

"We need to free the gnomes, Your Majesty," Queen Titania cried, clutching the king's sleeve.

"I agree, my sweet. Guard, call for the Prince of Gnomes if you will."

"Yes, Your Majesty," the guard answered. With a smart bow, he strode away.

"Are you hungry, Sugarplum?" the king asked, offering her a bowl of sweet cherries.

"Your Majesty, as much as I would like to eat, we have no time. All Hallows' Eve is upon us and I fear that Evilla and Dreadmore may execute their plan at any time."

"Yes, quite right." He turned as the Prince of Gnomes entered the room. "Prince Demone, thank-you for coming. A warlock has been changing gnomes to stone. What do you have that could change your brothers back from stone to gnome?"

"Your Majesty, to save many gnomes, you need a gnome ring of blue onyx enchanted with an emancipate spell cast upon it."

"Do you mean a liberty spell?"

"Yes, Your Majesty."

"That should work nicely. Do you have one?"

"Yes, Your Majesty. The problem is, Your Majesty, only master gnomes can use it. Gerome is our master gnome."

"That is indeed a problem. How can we free Gerome so he can use it to save the others?"

Demone thought for a moment. "Fairies know enough magic to save one, I think."

"You have to be sure, Prince Demone."

"I can provide a single potion that he could use," the prince replied.

"I think it's a she in this case," the king said, glancing at Sugarplum.

"Of course, Your Majesty. Excuse me, milady." Prince Demone bowed to Sugarplum. "I will get right on it sire." With that, he bowed once more and hurriedly left the hall.

"I sense something very evil going on here," said the Queen. "More than the normal pranks played at this time of year."

"I believe you are right, my dear, something extremely evil. Much more than just making Halloween evil again," answered the king. "Changing gnomes into stone, freezing scarecrows, and using magic potions on pumpkins tells me there is a lot more to it. Much more." He paused. "And what's with all the weasels? Where would they get that many weasels? Why do they need the weasels?"

"If it's just to scare children, they could have done that by flying on their brooms and screeching in the night! With faces grey with morbid evil, they would scare a ghost, let alone human children!" Queen Titania said, thinking out loud.

"I agree, so why all this trouble?"

"It does seem strange, Your Majesty," agreed Sugarplum. "Is there anything my friends and I could do to find out?"

"Keep an eye on the despicable pair, especially as tonight is Halloween.

And when you free Gerome, find out more about this potion the witch used on the pumpkins. As a master magic elf, he would know what it is, I'm sure."

"Yes, Your Majesty."

"And for our friends, make sure they get something a little extra at Christmas and Easter." The king smiled at Sugarplum.

"Of course, Your Majesty! But first, we have to fight the witch."

"Work before pleasure," he agreed with a nod.

Sugarplum spun on a sparkling toe and dashed from the room in a spray of sugar.

"My beautiful queen," King Oberon said, "I have grave concerns. I think this is more than just pumpkin stealing. There is greater evil here."

"Yes, Your Majesty, I believe you are right. These two have indeed grown in the black arts. They have hidden themselves away for many years and now it appears they are ready to unleash their wickedness. I have never forgotten what they did to me and now, after what they have done to sweet Sugarplum…"

The king stood to his feet. "They may try to open a gateway to the underworld or unleash some kind of devilish creature. We must stop them once and for all."

"As much as I hate to harm any creature, I do not believe these two will ever change."

"Unfortunately so my dear, unfortunately so….".

Back in his workshop, Prince Demone searched for the Liberty Spell potion ingredients scroll, nimbly maneuvering through the narrow passageways, around tall stacks of papers, magic books, and scrolls. He rummaged through the cubbyholes of his old roll-top desk, rifled through old manuscripts and tomes, and finally found it. In a drawer of a very old desk, almost completely hidden by even more stacks of manuscripts, there it lay.

"Aha! Here it is. Always in the last place you look. Now let me see," he muttered. His old assistant, Semone, dipped a quill into an inkwell then continued scribbling formulas on a curling sheet of parchment.

"May I be of assistance, Your Highness?"

"No, no, Semone. I found what I was looking for."

The prince ran down the spiral staircase, rushed past the kitchens, and raced through the storage cellar and into the tunnels leading into the heart of the mountain. He needed to find just the right minerals for the liberty potion. From the miners working below, he received mercury from the lava flows, copper from a mineshaft and gold flakes from the underground streams.

He rechecked his list. "Now, what else do I need?" He dashed outside the palace toward the shores of the enchanted lake. Albino mushrooms grew only in deep caves; he also needed mosses from under the magic waterfall, and shavings from the ancient ebony tree.

Once he had collected his ingredients, he rushed back to his workshop to put them together. Checking his scroll, he ground and mixed just the right amounts of the components and added a pinch of magic fairy dust.

He pumped the furnace bellows and brought the fires to red-hot heat then he fired the concoction until it became a golden liquid.

The moment of truth, he thought, his muscles taut. "A little cobalt…" He sprinkled in just the right amount. "…And a sprinkle of magnesium," he said. His tongue slipped out between his lips to help him to concentrate. "Now for the dangerous part." Shaking just a little and dripping with sweating, he added the last few drops of his secret ingredient, nitro glycerin.

The liquid began to glow, and then it rumbled, turned orange then blue. Steam rolled over the edges of the pot. The prince blotted his brow with his handkerchief and held the container steady. Ever so carefully, he poured the charmed liquid into a vial. Just as it started to bubble and boil over, he popped a cork into the top so as not to lose any of its potency. He closed his eyes and prayed that it would not explode. Seconds ticked by. No blast. He opened one eye then the other.

"Whew, thank goodness that worked," he puffed. "I don't think the king would appreciate his palace blown to smithereens!"

"I wouldn't want to be blown to smithereens, either," said Semone's voice from behind a stack of papers.

"Now for the Blue Onyx ring," the prince continued. Putting his index finger to his brow, he thought out loud. "Now where in Fairyland did I put that ring?"

Once again he began rummaging frantically through huge cupboards and pulling open drawers.

"Semone!" he called for his assistant. "I need the rings!"

"I'm coming, Your Highness!" From behind a large desk came a bespectacled gnome still wearing a jeweler's glass, a visor, and an apron.

"I know it's here somewhere. The king needs the ring of Blue Onyx."

"Ah, the liberty ring. We have a few folks frozen in stone do we?"

"Yes. Now help me find that flaming ring."

"Now you want a flaming ring? I thought you wanted the liberty ring. If you want a flaming ring then I need to look in the rubies?"

"I do, I do, just help me find the ring!"

"The Liberty… or the Flaming?"

"The Blue Onyx!" he yelled.

"Yes, Your Highness," he sniffed.

"Hmmm, let me see," mumbled Semone as he fumbled through a large card index back at his desk. Stored in the cupboards and drawers, curios, and display cases of the workshop, placed on hooks hung rows and rows, were all kinds of magical jewelry and artifacts. "Bracelets of invisibility, no, necklaces of persuasion, no, amulets of speed, no, lockets of love potions, oh my dear, no."

"Aha! Here they are… rings," Prince Demone shouted as he opened a large drawer in an antique curio cabinet.

"Very good, Your Highness."

There must have been a thousand rings in the drawer. Each one held in its setting a different coloured gem. Each had been made for a different magical purpose, enabling the wearer to cast or use speed, fire, storms of winter, or dark shadows. There was a ring for almost anything one could imagine, all neatly displayed in impeccable order by Semone.

"Now let me see…" Prince Demone had no time for searching and frantically tossed rings aside while Semone attempted to catch them and put them back in place.

"Ruby, no, yellow topaz, no, blue sapphire, warmer but no, emerald, no, no. Where is the Blue Onyx?" he said leaning on a large gem box. "I need the Blue Onyx!"

"You're leaning on it," Semone intoned, gazing at the ceiling.

"Oh, he-he, thank-you, Semone," the prince said. "You can go back to your work now."

"Yes, Your Highness." He surveyed the disheveled cupboards and drawers, open jewelry boxes and misplaced gems. "I will get right on it," he said with a deep sigh.

Carefully carrying the vial up and the ring box the castle stairs, Prince Demone raced to the palace gate where Sugarplum hovered waiting for him.

"Be very careful, Sugarplum. This is no ordinary potion."

"Thank you, Prince Demone..."

"Don't shake it. It may explode!"

Ever so carefully, she placed it in her pouch for safekeeping.

"Good luck, Sugarplum!" the prince called after her as she flew away toward a portal.

Bruce Kilby

Bruce Kilby

# Chapter 14

# The Day of Haunting

Halloween day started much like most fall days in Weasel Warren. Cool, brisk air ensured little warmth from the sun that arose a little later and a little lower each day. On the farm, just as on most days, many of the chores had already been finished. Daisy and her sisters had been milked and put out to pasture, what few eggs there were had been collected, and the goats and sheep had been shooed out of the hay barn by Mrs. McSimmons. Molly and Barley had clean stalls, strewn with fresh hay; the pigs had their feed of daily slop and of course, the crows had been scared away from the last remaining apples in the orchard by Sneezer and Farmer McSimmons.

As in past years, Henrietta and the hens had trouble laying eggs the morning after the petting zoo incident but now, the added stress from hearing the early fireworks going off in and around Weasel Warren made it even more difficult. In fact, many of the farm animals had slept little over the past few nights fearing the boom, crackle, or whizzing sounds caused by impatient teens setting off fireworks. Each night the sky was alive with strange sparkling lights and fast moving missiles that exploded, sounding like Farmer McSimmons' fire stick.

The animals never understood humans. Even Duke had abandoned Rapture Ridge as the teens gathered there. Now, instead of eating or pressing faces together, they lit off fireworks and that scared him more than even Patches' whirlybirds.

"Sugarplum! It's so nice to see you back!" Quacks squealed. "Unfortunately, I have just finished breakfast. A little sugar would have been nice on top of my apples." He pouted his disappointment.

"I went to see Oberon, King of the Fairies and Queen Titania, to give them back the amulet. Now Dreadmore won't be changing any more gnomes into stone."

"Ahh, that is a good thing."

"King Oberon and the Queen thank you, all of you, for helping me. They were so pleased."

"No problem," Stranger said entering the nest with Pronto at his heels.

"Well, tonight's the night," Quacks continued. "Whatever that witch has planned is going down but what? The question is still unanswered."

"Very true," Sugarplum agreed. "King Oberon would like us to keep an eye on the witch and warlock and free Gerome the Gnome. He thinks that he may be able help figure out what she is up to. He's our best hope."

"How do we do that?"

"Prince Demone, Prince of Gnomes gave me this liberty potion before I left. I am to use it on Gerome. It should release the spell."

"Well, dere's no time like da present," Stranger stated.

Quacks got up from his comfy nest and donned his Captain's hat. On their way to Mrs. McSimmons front yard, Sneezer joined the group just to be nosey, even though he didn't know what was going on. He was the farm guard dog after all. He was tired after spending half the night licking his wounds clean.

They found the statue of Gerome in his usual stationary spot beside the wishing well. He wore a bright red cap, a long grey beard, a bright blue vest over a white shirt. His red trousers matched his hat.

Sneezer sniffed him and looked in the statue's eyes for any sign of life but gnome just returned his perpetually lifeless stare. Lifting his leg he heard a chorus of "Nooooo!" from behind him and lowered it again.

Sugarplum flew over the statue and gently brought out the tiny vial. "I would stand back if I were you," she said to the group, "especially you Sneezer. I am not sure what kind of mood Spell Master Gerome might be in after such a long time."

They had moved back to a safe distance away as she carefully poured the vial's contents over Gerome's head.

"POOOF!" A small, blue cloud appeared then disappeared. The magical liquid dripped down over Gerome's head and dribbled its way down. In a moment, the statue began rocking back and forth and vibrating. The stone cap turned back into wool cloth, the stone beard into hair and the body changed from rock to live gnome. In seconds Gerome had been transformed back into his real live gnome.

He snarled and snorted then wheezed and gulped in the fresh air for the first time in years. He was not happy, not happy at all.

"I need a shower!" he hollered in a heavy brogue accent. Giving Sneezer a long scornful look, he marched straight to the well and began pumping the handle. Standing under its waterfall he spluttered, "Everyday! That thing..." he pointed an accusing finger at Sneezer, "did his business...on me!"

Sneezer lowered his head and sidled behind Quacks.

"Can you believe it? A Master Gnome being used that way? I have never been so humiliated!" Crossing his arms tapped his foot and scowled as the fresh water dripped off of him.

"I tried to warn you," Sugarplum whispered to Sneezer.

Duke dropped from the sky and landed on the roof over the well. "Caw, caw, caw," he laughed. "He's mad. Mad, mad, mad. Caw."

Sugarplum snickered.

Quacks chuckled.

Pronto giggled then they all broke out in belly laughs.

Even Gerome managed a wry smile, thankful he had been finally released from his granite prison. Stretching out his arms he gaped at the colour of his clothing. "Who in the suffering tarnation did this to me?!" he roared.

"Not me! Definitely not me!" Sneezer yelped.

"I cannot be seen in this! I am not a clown. I'm a gnome! This will not do. It will not do at all."

"That was Mrs. McSimmons idea," Quacks explained. "She thought you looked nicer standing in the garden painted in bright colours." Duke squawked with laughter again.

"Humph!" he grunted jamming his hands on his hips. "Humans are mad. Next they'll want take me on holidays to take pictures with me! Displayed like a leprechaun!" His head wagged from side to side. "Sometimes I just don't know."

"Aye, I believe this hag and her henchman need to be taught a lesson!" Gerome agreed after drying himself on Sneezer's doghouse blankets. "One minute I am helping the Mother Nature; the next minute I wake up dressed like clown having been tinkled on...every day! I thought I had done something wrong and was being punished."

"King Oberon had the Prince of Gnomes make you this Blue Onyx ring. It holds an Emancipation Spell," Sugarplum said handing the ring to Gerome. "Now you can free all of the gnomes."

"It looks like I have a huge job in front of me freeing all of the gnomes in the world. There could be thousands, millions!" He slipped the ring on his right index finger.

"The King also thought you might know what the witch plans to do with the pumpkins," ventured Sugarplum.

"Aye, a little strange it is. Let me think about it." Rubbing his chin, he thought for a long moment. "Wait a minute...you said she was making some kind of potion. Do you have any idea what she put in that potion?"

"I heard 'a witch's mole'." Stranger offered right away.

"Yes, that was the last ingredient," Sugarplum agreed with a nod.

"What else did she put in it, my dear?" Gerome pressed.

"Oh. I remember," Sugarplum said, clapping her hands. "Before that she added phantom's foot and a ghouls tongue. I think that's it."

"Are you sure, little one? It doesn't seem quite right. There should be more. Think hard, as hard as you can."

Pronto ran in between them and tugged on Gerome's short pants, snarling like a wolf and pretending to bite Stranger's neck.

"Oh yes," Sugarplum gasped. "Thank-you, Pronto. She added Jaws of a Werewolf."

"That's good. Anything else?"

"What's a Werewolf?" Stranger muttered. "I never heard of dat in da big city."

"I need to know all the ingredients if I'm going to get this right," Gerome continued.

"Vampire blood. At least I think so…"

"Yup, sounds right to me," Stranger added while Pronto nodded vigorously.

"Okay, let me see," Gerome said, tugging on his beard. "Phantoms foot—that's something to do with walking, ghouls tongue, hmm, shrieking maybe. Jaws of a Werewolf—biting, definitely biting. That's not good, not good at all, and Vampire's blood you say? Oh, oh."

"What do you mean 'Oh, oh'? Oh, ohs are never good," Stranger interrupted.

"Nope never good," agreed Sneezer.

"I believe it means she made a potion of living dead," Gerome announced.

"Living dead!" Quacks exclaimed.

"Yes, it raises the living dead. I'm sure that's it."

"We're doomed!" Stranger moaned.

"Don't forget the witch's mole!" Sugarplum added.

"Oh yes, that's just to make more evil, more ugly!" Gerome replied.

"If it ain't already!" said Stranger.

"I'm not one who's up on evil spells, that be f'sure, but it sounds to me that she's making a walking dead spell." Gerome's brow furrowed as he looked from face to face.

"Walking dead spell?!" they all gasped.

"Caw, don't like that, don't like that! Caw," Duke screeched as he sat on the rim of Sneezer's dog dish flapping his wings while eyeing the last remaining scraps in the bottom of the bowl. He never wanted to miss the chance of a meal.

"That be it, me thinks, and me thinks whatever they are, are gonna be quite vicious too!" Gerome added.

"Walking dead and vicious! That's all we need! Now what do we do?" Quacks asked, beginning to shake.

"Well, whatever it is, tonight's the night. It's All Hallows' Eve, the night evil plays," Gerome added somberly. "There's no time to make a Change Potion, I'll have to think of another way."

"It's too late to round up all the pumpkins. They've all been carved and placed on every doorstep all over town. They're ready to go." said Sneezer

"We gotta do somethin'," said Stranger.

"Stranger, Pronto, you two go keep an eye on the witch's house and those weasels," Quacks ordered, taking command. "See what they do next."

"Yes, Boss, er, I mean, Quacks!" Stranger saluted and smacked Pronto on the shoulder. "Let's go, little buddy."

"Gerome, you can start freeing your brothers around Weasel Warren and Badgerville but keep an ear to the ground as we may need you and your friends later. In fact, count on it."

"Aye, aye," said Gerome.

"Duke, ask your brothers if they could help us once more. I think we'll need them tonight to feed on a pumpkin or two."

"Caw, caw!" Duke squawked, bobbing his head.

"Sneezer, Sugarplum, and I will go into Weasel Warren in case these conniving vultures try to do something early. Come running if you hear the signal."

"What signal?" Sneezer asked.

"Your howl. It's loud enough to wake the dead!" Quacks said without thinking. They all stared at him. "What?" He glanced around. "Come on, you know what I mean."

Without complaint, they all took off in different directions toward their assigned destinations to wait and see what would happen next.

R.I.P.

Bruce Kilby

# Chapter 15

# The Hour of the Witch

In Weasel Warren, Badgerville, and all of the villages, towns, and cities, the preparations for Halloween were almost complete. The costumes were made or bought, the candy ready at the front door and the carved pumpkins placed on the front steps.

Excited children were all ready with their goody bag pillowcases, running around their yards wearing their masked disguises. There was the usual fare, those pretending to be various superheroes or the ever-popular pirate. There were princesses, witches, angels, ballerinas and bunnies. Sprinkled amongst the crowed was the odd scary mask of a wolf, skeleton, dinosaur, or a vampire or ghost. All anxiously waited for the sun to finally slip and hide once again behind the horizon.

As the day waned the first to move were the witch, warlock, and weasels. Out from the cottage, the witch and warlock flew low on their brooms while the weasels followed on foot. This time the weasels carried many wooden cages with them.

"Now what would dey be for?" Stranger muttered to Pronto from their familiar hiding spot in the bushes.

The procession started to make its way through the Northwoods and headed toward Weasel Warren.

"They should be lighting their pumpkins any time now," the witch cackled. "That will be our signal. My sweet darlings will awaken," she said to the evil laughter of the warlock.

Once the last weasel cleared out of the cottage, Stranger nudged Pronto. "You go on. Keep following 'em. Dere's something I gotta do."

Pronto looked up at his companion, puzzled. "What do you mean?"

"Don't worry, li'l buddy, I'll catch up." He turned and disappeared into the undergrowth.

With all of the weasel scouts about, Pronto scurried under leaves and through thatched grasses ad the procession made its way through the Northwoods.

Minutes later, Stranger caught up to Pronto. The procession had stayed in the Northwoods as long as they could, skirting the Tucker potato farm, Mr. Dhaliwal's blueberries, and Mr. Chang's ginger fields. Running through the ditches, they hid behind stone walls and under bridges.

Stranger and Pronto followed stayed close behind.

At the edge of town, the weasels dashed across the main road in small groups then crept through the church grounds until they finally reached their destination.

"Okay, boys, we'll wait here. This is perfect!" cackled the witch as they settled amongst the headstones of the Weasel Warren graveyard.

In ancient times this graveyard had been closer to the river but after a flood, some of the older parts had been swamped. Many moss-covered headstones tilted, half sunken in what was now the bog. Overgrown weeping willows and cypress trees drooping with lichen added to the eerie impression as the sunlight ebbed, casting long shadows, and the day turned to twilight.

"Why do we get all the scary jobs?" asked Pronto as they nestled behind a family crypt darkened with time and shrouded in moss. As mist rose off the damp swamp, he shivered.

"Dis is nuttin', Pronts. The way I look at it, it's better bein' on dis side of da daisies than pushin' dem up!"

Pronto, not calmed by this thought, looked around. "Yikes!" he squealed. He found himself staring directly into the stone face of a grave guardian meant to keep evil spirits away. He leapt to his feet and started to run.

Stranger grabbed him by the scruff of the neck. "Pronts! Stay alert and don't give us away. There's way too many of them." Stranger tucked the mouse in beside him.

"B-b-but, loooooook!"

Stranger looked up at the same gory face. "Yeah, yeah, I know. Don't much like him either. Stay with me, little buddy. We have to get closer to da action." The pair slunk through the shadows to another headstone downwind from the weasel hordes.

As the sun made its last orange streaks over the western horizon, the pumpkins on the steps lit up to signify that homes were ready to welcome little tricksters.

In the village, throngs of costumed children, escorted by a parent or two, ran out into the streets. Some travelled in ones and twos, others in small groups. "Trick or treat!" echoed all over the neighborhoods as the costumed masses rushed from house to house. Candies dropped into bags and clusters of children ran to the next house that had a pumpkin lit or porch light on.

"That looks easy," said Sneezer, licking his chops.

"Shhh, just keep your eyes on what's going on," warned Quacks, peering from their hiding spot under the town square bandstand gazebo.

It was Sugarplum who spotted the first stirring of the pumpkins. "Look!" she cried in a high-pitched whisper, pointing to the porch stoop of the nearest house.

Two grotesque spindly arms sprouted out from the pumpkin's sides then two gangly legs appeared under it. Once fully grown it staggered and stood up, arms waving to balance.

The candle inside its mouth grew brighter so its whole head radiated bright yellow orange. From each eye licks of flame belched out and from the fanged jaw a flaming tongue darted. The scary orbs were now alive.

They were no longer the decorative works of children's fantasies; they were now gruesome figments of horror.

"Look, look!" she exclaimed.

"Whoa!" said Quacks, alarmed at what he saw.

The glowing head started snapping its jaw and waving its arms as it stepped down from the porch, heading for the front yard gate.

The next group of children entering the yard screamed, dropped their bags of candies and rushed back to hide their faces behind their parents at the gate.

At first, some laughed assuming it was part of the decorations, a ruse to scare the children as they came up to the door but their smiles vanished when they saw that one, then another, then several more pumpkins on the block came alive. With a clumsy walk, wood-like arms and spindly fingers extended, the pumpkins were now after them!

"Now we move, my darling," the witch cackled as she gazed over the village.

She and the warlock took off on their brooms. Swooping over the graveyard, they pulled out vials from within secret pockets in their black cloaks. Once uncorked, they poured more of their hideous cauldron goo onto the graves. As each drop landed, the earth hissed and smoked, and sizzled as it plopped into the murky swamp water.

"He, he, he, rise my beauties, rise, rise!" she crowed with hysterical glee.

Under the watchful eyes hidden in the shadows, several long seconds passed until finally the ground started to rumble. The mounds of dirt shook then began to crack, and then heave outward from below. Skeletal fingers began to appear, followed by whole hands that reached up and clawed their way through to the surface.

"Good, good, my darling!" cried the warlock.

"Dat's not good!" Stranger whispered. "Not good at all."

Pronto had been gobbling sunflower seeds to calm his nerves, leaving a pile of shells around his feet. He nodded his head vigorously in agreement while quivering in fear.

Breaking away from the blanket of earth, several old skeletons stood up. With their clothes long disintegrated, the boney figures began to unsteadily walk around, testing their bony legs. For many, it had been centuries since they had felt solid ground under foot.

Next, one then two, then a dozen ghouls with flesh still dangling from their bones arose. Eyeballs dangled from their grey faces and sprigs of remaining hair hung from their heads. They still wore the funeral clothes, now ragged and dusty, in which they had been buried. As if a time capsule had been opened, the different styles of clothes worn over the centuries that had not yet disintegrated appeared.

Zombies with tri-corn hats and white wigs, nineteenth century top hats and tuxedos, even those wearing military uniforms arose from the older places of eternal rest. Dragging unused legs and hobbling awkwardly, they groaned and lurched to join the gathering of skeletons.

With no bones remaining at all, wispy ghosts, wraiths and banshees came up from the ancient graves and flew in circles amidst the monster horde. Their screams and howls of protest from being awoken from their eternal rest added to the scary chaos as they flew through the thickening ground mist.

"And I thought cities were scary!" Stranger whispered to Pronto. The two friends now quaked with fear as they looked on from behind a statue of a peaceful angel. Pronto tried to bolt once more but Stranger firmly stood on his tail allowing no means of escape.

Even with all that was going on in front of them, Stranger sensed something else. Something eerie. He looked over his shoulder toward a strange gurgling sound bubbling up from the dank stagnant ponds.

"Now what?"

Evilla and Dreadmore, the skeletons, ghouls and ghosts all froze and turned to see where the sound was coming from. Even the skeletons and ghouls half out of their crypts stopped clawing at the earth.

Long-buried coffins broke from the muck and bobbed to the surface. Before long the whole swamp lay covered in floating coffins.

Both Stranger and Pronto watched in horror as they waited and listened. Long seconds passed before the first thump was heard from within a casket. The sounds of scratching and clawing came from others until dripping boney fists punched through their decaying wooden tops. Skeletons dressed like pirates covered in green slime and dripping with swamp water stood in up the floating coffins. As if by command, each drew his cutlass and flintlock pistol and turned his skull to await the order from the witch.

"You got to be kiddin' me!" Stranger gasped in disbelief.

"Oh, my evil beauties," Evilla squealed in delight. "Even the long lost crew of Red Beard, the Pirate, the most notorious pirate on the Spanish Main? They killed over five hundred men! How lucky can a girl get!" she cackled.

"My dear, I think it's time," Dreadmore crooned.

"Yes, yes, my sweet," she replied with glee. "Time to walk the night! Time to take back what is ours! Walk, walk, my legion of the night! Walk!" she howled, pointing toward the town.

Clacking their teeth or moaning in misery and pain, the mangled mass of the walking dead stumbled, limped, and dragged unused legs toward the cemetery entrance and the center of town. Those who had been buried in armor or had carried swords now clanked, rattled their weapons, beat upon their shields, or dragged chains over granite gravestones. This was their night and after all this time, they were ready to take back what was once theirs.

When the first group of tricksters saw what was coming out of the graveyard, they giggled thinking the older teens had dressed in some really cool costumes.

"They look real," said one little boy.

"So cool," said another.

That all stopped when one of the wraiths spiraled around a boy and screamed in his face. A ghost walked right through a young girl while a banshee cried its high-pitched haunting cry above. The youngsters' faces changed to that of utter terror as they screamed and ran for their lives.

Windows thumped closed, doors slammed shut, and front porch lights winked out. Dogs barked until they saw what was approaching then yelped in fear and ran as fast as they could to hide under whatever they could find. Children scattered while parents scrambled to scoop them up in their arms. Like a school of fish before a shark attack, people fled in all directions to escape the oncoming host.

"Get them!" Evilla shrieked, pointing at the slowest moving families.

The cadaverous army of the living dead marched on into town, groaning, screeching, and grasping with a slow, steady awkward stumble led by the apparitions, the ghosts, wraiths, and banshees, now encircling and running through the scattering villagers.

"EEEEEEK!" a lady screamed and ran when a ghost jumped out of the door she was about to enter.

There was no escaping the tide of terror rounding up the parents.

"It looks like hell has opened its gates!" cried Sugarplum.

"I think you might be right," Quacks answered, his eyes popping from their sockets. "Yes, you might be right."

RIP
RIP

Bruce Kilby

# Chapter 16

## Something More Evil Going On

With all the commotion, no one had noticed one last coffin rising to the murky surface back in the cemetery. This one was very different from the others that lay strewn about broken open from the inside. This ominous casket was rusty and made from cast iron and wrapped, then rewrapped in chains. Large iron nail heads rimmed the casket through the double-layered box. It was certain, that whoever had buried this coffin never wanted whatever was inside to leave, ever.

"Oh, oh!" Stranger muttered as Pronto stared wide-eyed.

Pounding started from within. Whatever was inside desperately wanted out.

BOOM! BOOM! BOOM!

Bulges began to appear in the top of the coffin from the blows. The unnerving sounds of clawing and moaning from within the box rang through the chill night air. Chains buckled and iron links creaked.

"Yikes! This don't look good," whispered Stranger. "Stop eatin' da spits and git goin'. Ya better go tell Quacks." He lifted his foot to release Pronto's tail.

Like a bullet, Pronto streaked off, heart pounding. Happy he did not have to stay and face whatever was in the box. But just as he reached the cemetery entrance archway, he screeched to a halt. With second thoughts he turned toward his friend and called out in a hoarse whisper, "Are you sure? I don't want to leave you alone here."

"Don't worry about me, little buddy, I can deal with this," Stranger said more bravely than he felt. "Now go!"

Tiny Pronto was hardly noticed weaving in and out of the weasels, ghouls, and skeletons in town. One wraith came down to him and stared at him with black soulless eyes but his orders were to scare humans, not little field mice. Pronto once again gathered up what little of he had left of his courage and headed toward Quacks. When he reached the edge of the town square he heard the witch, screeching overhead.

"It won't be long now my beauties!" she howled to the weasels, "Bring up the cages!"

Back at the cemetery, Stranger no longer wanted to wait to see what was trying to break out of the chained coffin. Maybe, just maybe, this thing was too big for even a tough city raccoon like him to handle. Maybe dose chains will hold, he hoped, and decided it might be safer to leave the graveyard and follow Pronto. He loped toward the cemetery entrance. Suddenly, behind him he heard the ringing snap of iron chains breaking followed by the ear-splitting creak of rusty hinges. Crouching behind a tilting headstone, eyes wide, he saw the chains wrapping the casket fall away into the swamp water and the lid of the coffin rise.

Frozen with fear, Stranger saw a huge set of human-like bones begin to climb out of its rusty crypt. Long arms with hands joined to long, bony fingers reached upward. Slowly the creature stood up in the iron casket revealing a barrel-like chest cavity. The beast lifted the hollow eyes in its massive skull toward the full moon and snapped his long razor sharp teeth together. Stranger thought the creature had tried to howl but he heard no sound but the clattering of its mighty jaws.

Now bathed in the full moon light, his skeletal body started to transform. Skin began to form over his head and body, inhuman eyes reformed in his skull; bright yellow centres lit the deathly black eyeballs. Next, hair sprouted on the face, arms, and down his legs. Even in the back alleys where Stranger had come from, he had never seen such a beast.

The huge monster hunched over and his knees snapped backward becoming like an animal's hind legs. His fingers elongated into claws and his head transformed into the most gruesome wolf Stranger had every witnessed. Wiry fur now completely covered the creature's body, and his teeth lengthened into ghastly fangs.

Suddenly, the being clutched his neck as though he'd felt a searing pain. A puff of smoke rose from where his paw ripped away the remains of a garlic clove necklace and silver cross. He looked up, reached his outstretched arms to the moon and howled.

"Awoooooooooooooo! Awooooooooooooo!"

Throughout the village, a shudder of fear ran through the streets and heads snapped around in the direction of the ghastly bay.

'Dis ain't good, not good at all! Stranger thought. He crouched lower behind the tombstone but it was too late. He had been discovered.

The beast sniffed the acrid night air as though he had caught the scent of a living animal. Stranger sensed, he didn't know how, that the creature hungered for fresh meat after being imprisoned for so long in his iron tomb. It was true that the fiend needed living blood to run through his veins once more and anything would do, as long as it was still breathing.

Stranger sprang from his hiding place and darted in and out of the rows of gravestones. Slipping behind a statue, he hoped his fur's markings would disguise him in the shadows just as they had many times in the big city while escaping the animal catchers. In those days, he just sat motionless high in a fir tree and watched his pursuers search for him below. Once they were gone he went on his merry way in another direction.

Snarling and gnashing his teeth, the beast leapt from gravestone to gravestone. He took a swipe with his claws at the very spot Stranger had been, but found air. Two quick bounds and the beast flew to the roof of a mausoleum, howled again and sniffed the air for that living blood.

Stranger clenched his teeth and tried not to breathe but it was no use. As if he could hear the pounding of Stranger's heart, the beast sprang toward Stranger's hiding spot, crushing the gravestone to dust with his weight.

"Awoooooooooooooo!" the beast howled in disappointment after missing his prey yet again.

Stranger, now flushed out into the open, ran faster than he had ever run before. He had always relied on his cunning to evade enemies and had never been a fast runner. He knew that even though he was out of shape and out of breath, he had to run now, for his life.

The beast came on relentlessly. Stranger had never been pursued like this before. By now a dog would have given up, or Stranger could have climbed a tree to escape but this beast was different. A tree would provide no shelter from the ravenous rage and razor like claws.

As the snarls and growls grew closer, Stranger darted this way and that using all the tricks he had learned in the big city to escape the pound. Dodging left, feint right then dodge left again. Turn a corner fast but stop so the hunter would pass then run the other way. The beast was never fooled for long.

Stranger could almost feel the hot, fowl breath upon him. Blindly, he turned sharply and darted into a dark, narrow gap between two crypts as the swipe of the clawed paw narrowly missed him as it too reached into the gap. Now sure that he was out of reach, Stranger grasped his heaving chest and squatted.

Meanwhile in the village, the Weasel Warren Warlock flew over the crowds pointing his staff at the children and firing his perfected change spell. Poof! He changed a child into a weasel! Poof! Poof! Another and another. "I'm the Weasel Warren Warlock and I'm coming after you!" he sang cheerily.

By the time Pronto had found Quacks and mimed that the approaching ghouls, the ghosts and skeletons were almost upon them. Quacks saw the children being herded by the pumpkins toward the warlock and the parents being separated and chased by the un-dead. The situation was bad and they were in deep, deep trouble.

Like an army, the pumpkins marched down the street, snapping, snarling, and spitting flames as they drove the children into groups beneath the Warlock.

"We cannot stop this," Quacks squealed. "All hell has broken out! We need help right away. Sneezer howl, howl like you've never howled before!"

"Oooooowwwwwwwww!" Sneezer bayed.

"Louder, louder," yelled Quacks.

"OOOOWWWWWW! OOOOWWWWWW!"

"Good boy! Keep it up!" Quacks commanded. "Sugarplum, find Gerome. We need his help! Find any more gnomes he may have freed, too!"

Sugarplum took off in a glittering flash, flying through unsuspecting specters and making sure to avoid the witch. Her sparkling trail of light disappeared on its way to Badgerville.

"Wadda you doin' here?" a familiar voice sounded in the dark of the graveyard.

"Who's dat?" Stranger peered into the inky blackness, still trying to catch his breath in his hiding place between the two mausoleums.

"Punce Stincattio, of course. Don't you recognize your Italiano friend?"

As his eyes adjusted, Stranger could see the luminescence of the white fur and black stripe of his friend.

"Oh, Punk," Stranger gasped, yanking his old friend deeper into the crevice. "We gotta stop meetin' like dis." Stranger threw his arms around his stinky friend while keeping one eye on the beast recklessly ripping the crypts apart, brick by brick.

"Can't say it's good to see ya with that thing chasing ya," Punce replied, gently pushing Stranger away.

"Wadda ya doin' here?" Stranger asked. The beast flung away another brick.

"I was heading back to the big city," he answered hurriedly. "I thought I'd get a meal before I made my way. It's a long trek back to the city."

"Well," Stranger said, "ya picked a bad time for dat."

"Maybe, maybe not."

"We ain't got much time before dat thing gonna rip us apart." Stranger said nervously. "We got nowhere else to hide."

"Remember when I fell into that vat of chemicals and turned my black fur white and my white fur black?"

"Yeah."

"Well, it affected my scent glands too. When I tag, even I can smell it."

"A skunk who can smell his own spray? So what?"

"Maybe I can buy us some time."

"Wadda ya planin' to do?"

"Get ready to run." Punk lifted his tail, turned his rear toward the werewolf aimed, letting out a foul blast of skunk spray.

The wolf creature took a great swipe at the two huddled animals but his great paw stopped in mid-air just as he was about to connect. The wolf's hair went limp, his ears sank, and his eyes crossed. He gagged and spluttered as the putrid smell hit his nostrils.

"Run!" shouted Punk. "Ruuuuuuuun!"

Stranger didn't stop to think but ran toward the angel he had hidden behind before. As he scurried under her wing, he noticed a small blue bottle in her closed right hand. He jumped up into her arms and grabbed the vial with his tiny front paws.

"Maybe this can help," he cried even though he couldn't read the label that read, Holy Water.

When the revolting skunk smell began to clear, the beast shook his head, uncrossed his eyes and took in a huge gasp of fresh air. He gazed into the crack between the crypts and found his prey missing. Punk had gone one way while Stranger had gone another. He roared and gazed around, dazed. Sniffing, he located Stranger huddled in the arms of the stone angel. From his perch on the crypt wall, he leapt toward the raccoon with renewed frenzy.

Something in Stranger's heart told him what he had to do. He pawed the bottle upright, clutched it, and then chewed on the cork as fast as he could, desperate to open it before the werewolf reached him.

The beast landed in front of the statue, keeping his distance as he slunk toward his prey. He snarled a hideous growl, lowered his head, and hunkered onto his haunches. Stranger knew that the beast could see him struggling with the little bottle and watched in horror as the creature lunged. With his claws outstretched and with razor teeth flared, he sprang into the air.

Scrambling frantically, Stranger finally uncorked the vial. As the fanged jaws and claws leapt straight at him, he recklessly tossed its contents at the lunging beast.

"Awoooooooooooo!" The werewolf screamed, clawing at its eyes. He landed hard on the stone platform of the angel, past Stranger and the statue. He roared as though in intense pain or fury.

Stranger didn't waste a second. He had scrambled down from the angel and ran for his life.

As he streaked between the headstones and open crypts, Punk caught up to him and waddled as fast as he could in step with Stranger.

"Thanks, Punk," Stranger gasped as the two ran for the cemetery gate.

"No problem," his striped friend wheezed. "Which way?"

"I think this way," Stranger replied and scampered toward a tree near the cemetery wall.

Hearing the screams of pain behind them, they took a last look back at the squirming beast rubbing his eyes. For one brief moment, Stranger thought he saw the stone angel appear to smile then in the same moment return to her solemn guard over the tomb.

With no time to lose, they scuttled over the fence and out of the graveyard.

"Awoooooooooooow!" Another piercing wail echoed throughout the darkness.

Bruce Kilby

Bruce Kilby

# Chapter 17

# Good vs. Evil

"Down the halls and up the walls, I'm coming after you," the warlock sang while zapping fleeing children.

Sleazel, Diesel, and several other weasels followed the warlock, twisting in and out between the demented pumpkins and greedily stuffing children into wooden cages.

The witch cackled hysterically as she swooped in circles above the creatures. "This night is mine; it is the hour of the witch! The hour of pure evil! Look at my darlings, Darling," she cried as she surveyed the sight before her. Pumpkins rounded up children while ghouls, ghosts, and skeletons pursued the parents.

"Yes, my dear," the warlock answered. "It's a truly glorious site indeed!"

Stranger and Punk caught up to the group in the town square just as Sneezer, Pronto, and Quacks began attacking pumpkins to try and free the children.

Without hesitation they jumped into the fray. Punk grabbed a sprinkler hose lying on the lawn while Stranger raced to the gardener's shack and, with his nimble fingers, cranked on the tap.

With the sprinkler head spitting out water in circular streams, Punk got his face splashed each time the stream rotated. Fighting a skunk's natural dislike for water, he aimed the spray at the pumpkin heads, knocking off heads and putting out the flaming eyes and flaring mouths of others.

Despite their valiant efforts, for each child the heroes saved from the pumpkins' grasp, two or three more were changed into weasels by the warlock!

"Get them!" the witch shrieked when she saw the aqueous attack.

As a unit, the pirate skeletons clanked and rattled after Punk and Stranger and attacked with cutlasses drawn. Moving like a machine the pirates slashed the hose in pieces while others chased the rescuers.

Punk dropped the sprinkler head and ran, joining with his friends while the pirates returned to robotically rounding up parents.

"Got to talk to ya, Boss! It's really important!" Stranger tried to get Quacks' attention while fending off a deranged pumpkin.

"So this was their big plan!" Quacks gasped as he rolled over a smashed pumpkin. "Not only are they making Halloween evil again but they're changing all the children to weasels!"

"But Boss, dere's more."

"If we can't stop this, Evilla and |Dreadmore can change all of the children of the world into weasels! Halloween will only be for the walking dead and children of the night!" Quacks panted.

"But dere is something else!" yelled Stranger snapping a pirate's skeletal leg. "And it ain't gonna be pretty!"

"Can't you see I'm busy?" Quacks replied as he back-kicked a pumpkin into a wall, smashing it to pieces.

"Let me at 'em, let me at 'em!" Sneezer woofed, snapping a pumpkin's arm.

The ghosts, ghouls, and skeletons continued their slow stumbling and awkward walk, backing the adults into their homes. Some townsfolk took refuge in parked cars but were promptly hounded out by screaming banshees. Parents reaching for their children met with firing muskets and slashing swords of the pirates.

Ignoring the desperate pleas of the parents, each child was systematically taken, transformed, and stuffed into a cage.

One weeping mother broke through the line and scooped up her child only to see him change into a weasel, hiss at her, and jump from her arms.

Any weasels not carrying cages attacked the animals. They attacked from every direction, all at once! They knew that no matter how tough the animals were, there was no way they could hold them off for long.

As the groups of screaming, terrified children grew smaller and smaller, Stranger and Sneezer relentlessly bit and snapped the legs off the pumpkins while at the same time fighting off the attacking weasels.

Driven by the evil force within them, even with a limb or leg snapped off the crazed pumpkins still crawled after their prey. Disconnected limbs twitched and jerked before the last of the evil life force left it. Bewitched pumpkins, grasping, snapping, and belching fire, kept coming and coming.

"How many pumpkins did Farmer McSimmons have anyway?" gasped Quacks as he looked at the oncoming army.

"But dis is really important!" Stranger protested snapping another arm.

"Where did Punk go?" yelled Quacks, oblivious to Stranger.

"Maybe he took off!" Sneezer huffed.

"I wouldn't blame him if he had," Stranger replied.

Quacks tried to protect a few huddled children by ramming the approaching flame-spitting pumpkins with hid bulky body but he couldn't keep up his efforts long with weasels biting his ears and ankles.

Swooping overhead, the witch and warlock tasted victory. After all these years of planning, they tasted success within their grasp. They howled, screeched, and shrilled in glee. "See my darling Dreadmore? They are no match for us. We will have our victory!"

"There's one more," shouted the warlock as he zapped another child. "And another." Zap! He went back into his gleeful refrain, "I'm the Weasel Warren Warlock and I'm coming after you!"

Swooping down, he found a boy hiding behind a mailbox. The boy looked behind him but before he could escape, Dreadmore said, "Boo!" and zapped him, too.

Just as Quacks began to think that all was lost, he heard the sound of thousands of flapping wings. "Oh please, let it be them!" he prayed.

Out from the night sky, a living black throng dove into view. "Caw, caw," Duke shrilled along with all of the Northwoods' Skysquawker clan of crows. Joining them in the assault was one raven still wearing part of a chewed off chain around his ankle. The throng came thundering downward and attacked the pumpkins and weasels.

Using their claws and razor sharp beaks they ferociously set upon their targets with precise skill. The weasels screamed and let go of the children in their possession. Pieces of fur and pumpkin flew everywhere, out from the beating black mass.

Duke raised his sharp eyes and saw his friends and with several other crows broke off to help Quacks, Sneezer, and the others still fighting off the demonic creatures. The rest of the crows pecked at the ghouls and pirates who rattled and swiped at them with partial arms and hands.

The now free raven caught sight of the warlock and re-directed his attack at his evil captor, vehemently clawing and pecking at the villain's head. Distracted by the vengeance of the raven, the warlock could not reach his Staff of Change. At least for the moment, no more children would be turned into weasels!

"So that's where you went," said Pronto to a grinning, panting Stranger. "You freed the raven!" With that, Pronto zipped around three weasels so fast that their heads nearly twisted off.

"No time to pat ourselves on da back, Pronts. Dis ain't all we got comin'. There's somethin' more evil goin' on," Stranger explained, snapping another pumpkin's leg.

Pronto heard Stranger with real panic in his voice. "What do you mean, 'this ain't all we got comin','" Pronto demanded.

"Dat thing dat was banging on da coffin in da swamp."

"What was it?"

The horde of pumpkins around them mindlessly grasped and clutched at the children even while the crows pecked and feasted on them.

"It's big."

"Yeah, okay." Pronto frowned.

"It's hairy."

"Yeah, yeah." He tripped another pumpkin trying to escape the crow attack.

"It's scary," Stranger went on as he broke the arm off another pumpkin.

"What is it?!"

"Dunno!"

Pronto slapped his forhead. "What does it look like?"

A howl from the wolf creature screamed over the din of the fight. "Awoooooooooooo!"

"Dat. Half man, half wolf."

"Oh." Even Pronto's dark grey fur appeared to grow pale.

"What was that!" cried Quacks.

"I tried to tell ya, Boss."

"Oh my....," was all Quacks could manage. "Hell has indeed opened its gate."

The witched saw the beast making its way along the rooftops toward the village. "Look my darling Dreadmore," she cried with glee. "We have an unexpected guest. A wonderful, beautiful, delightful guest from the underworld!"

"The Demon Lord will be most happy with us!" the warlock answered excitedly. Finally, after so many years on this wretched world, our master will come, he thought, hungrily anticipating his reward.

The witch shrieked at her weasels. "Take my new slaves back to the woods! Take them! Take every last one of them!"

At the order, Sleazel, Diesel, and Meazel gave up their attack and flung with cages filled with squirming new weasels onto waiting carts while others lifted them on poles as if carrying prey on an African safari.

Just then another sound emerged from the din. "Charge!" Gerome the Gnome hollered as he burst into the town square. He and several other gnomes clung to the back of Molly the horse. Behind him, several others rode the back of galloping Barley the donkey.

Nobody had dared to ride Angus. He charged into the fray snorting and pawing anyway.

"Where's the war?" he bellowed.

"Yesssireee! Here comes the cavalry!" howled Sneezer, leaping like a pup.

Angus eyed all the orange pumpkins with their flaming eyes and mouths and saw red. With the same instincts as if he were in a bullring in Spain facing a Matador, he charged, crashing through their lines and tossing pumpkins in every direction. Tilting his horns left and right the gored pumpkins smashed to the cobblestones. He skidded to a stop with a flaming pumpkin lodged on one of his horns. A steaming snort bellowed from his nostrils as he swung his massive head with pride.

Shattered pumpkins littered the streets everywhere one looked.

"Good boy!" yelled Quacks. "Now see what you can do with the zombies!"

"Though I ride through the valley of the shadow of death..." Angus roared, stomped his hooves. He dipped his head and charged again. Rotting bodies and bones soared as he mowed down rows of ghouls and skeletons. The mangled body parts littered the street.

Arms hung from telephone lines, legs lodged in trees, and heads rolled down roof tops, still alive and attempting to crawl, scratch, and inch their way back to rejoin the rest of their owners. With crows tearing at flesh, stealing limbs, and pecking at their faces, ghouls and skeletons alike staggered to stand, attaching an arm or hand or turning a head to once again face forward. Once body parts had attached, they limped, hobbled, or dragged themselves to rejoin the repulsive mob of horror while the crows sustained their relentless attack.

Gerome pointed his glowing, pulsating, blue onyx liberty ring at one of the filled cages.

"Zapp!" A huge flash of blue aura streamed from his hand. The blue electrical bolt hit the weasels trapped inside the cage. Instantly, the frightened furry animals became little boys, causing the cage to burst wide open. Shaken and dazed the boys scrambled to their feet and checked themselves over.

Gerome zapped another and another and the stunned captives once again became children.

"Yes!" Quacks shouted with joy.

"Noooooooo!" howled the witch. "This cannot be!"

Next, floating unnervingly down the middle of the road to Badgerville, and followed by a long line of calm un-possessed pumpkins, came a cross-shaped figure silhouetted by the moon. Dressed in a long, ragged coat, a shabby fedora, and whirlybirds on his shoulders, the figure carried a scythe and called out, "Mine, mine, mine!"

Stranger recognized him right away. "Patches! Gerome must have freed dat ting, too! I knew it; I knew it. He is alive! I told ya he was alive, Duke!" he shouted at the startled crow.

The newcomer's patchwork face seemed to smile as he swooped in. With his outstretched arms he commanded, "My pumpkins, my pumpkins, I am the Guardian of the Pumpkin Patch and I command you to return and return you must!"

A green bolt of lightning split the sky and flashed through Patches' form, out through his pointed scythe, and struck a nearby pumpkin. The streak bounced from one pumpkin to another then another. As the green bolts ricocheted through the remaining pumpkins, their fiery faces went out, their arms went limp by their sides and exactly as ordered, they turned and joined the others from Badgerville. Under the influence of the green aura, they calmly followed Patches and began marching back in the direction of Farmer McSimmons' pumpkin patch.

"Hurray!" Quacks bellowed.

"Nooooooo!" shrilled the witch. "Not my darlings!"

She circled once again and along with the warlock, she pulled on the handle of her broom and swooped down to attack once more. "I will not be defeated! I WILL NOT!"

The other gnomes formed a circle and together fired all forms of Mother Nature missiles at the evil pair as they approached like jet fighters coming in low. One group of three conjured a huge ball of lightning and hurled it toward the menacing duo. When the bolt struck them, the witch and warlock lit up like an x-ray and veered away—a momentary delay that did not stop them.

Next, several gnomes flung hailstones that stung the attackers as they flew while others conjured a snowstorm! But each spell delayed them for only a brief moment. Their evil aura protected them like a shield.

"Come, my darlings," Evilla called to the un-dead. "Get these meddling fools! They annoy me."

The army of partially reconstructed pirates, ghouls, and skeletons turned on the gnomes while the wraiths furiously swirl amongst them.

Undeterred, the warlock hit the children once again and turned them back into weasels. As fast as Gerome was changing them into children,

Dreadmore zapped them back again. One girl changed into a weasel three times in quick succession leaving her staggering, dazed, and confused.

The onslaught started once more.

"Not again!" yelled Quacks. "We have to get that, that thing off of him." He pointed at Dreadmore's staff.

The gnomes continued to fire giant snowballs at the ghouls trudging doggedly toward them but again the missiles only slowed them down; they didn't stop them. The skeletons were a different matter. They instantly reformed after they were blasted apart, so their persistent march was delayed for only a few seconds each time. Molly and Barley kicked with their hind legs, smashing them apart only to see the bones reform again and again. Sneezer, Stranger, and even Pronto bit at their bones, tearing them apart but as soon as the pieces were strewn, they would reform from the feet up to the head. Once reformed, they continued their relentless assault. The gnomes tried freezing rain that froze them in place only to have the witch swoop down and shatter the ice with her broom. Nothing worked and they kept coming.

Angus charged once more barging though the bone armies like a bowling ball through marbles. Bones flew everywhere. Pieces of flesh-covered arms and legs scattered and Angus' hooves even smashed a few skulls but no matter how many he destroyed, even he could not stop them.

'Dis is hopeless!" cried Stranger.

"Tasty though," Sneezer replied, chewing on a wriggling bone.

Pronto rolled his eyes then spat spits in the face of a startled ghoul.

"I don't think we can to stop them," said Quacks, defeated.

As the ghouls started to grasp and clamp onto the band of warriors, Quacks knew they were running out of ideas and running out of time. Under his breath he wished, "Sugarplum, if you can hear me now, we need your help… NOW!"

"What the..?" Dreadmore shrilled as the pungent smell hit his nose forcing him to spiral and lurch. Using both his hands to hold on to his broom he dropped his Staff of Change.

"That smell! It's…it's awful!" screeched the witch paralyzed by the stench! "This is so…disgusting!" With all of her potions, elixirs, and concoctions, even she had never smelled a stench like this before.

Punk had climbed up to the top of the gazebo and tagged both the witch and warlock with his special spray. Stunned like rock and unable to function, they both turned their brooms upward to find fresh air.

"Way to go Punk!" yelled Stranger.

Now, without the witch and warlock, the ice delayed the creatures longer giving the defenders a chance. It was a small chance but a chance nevertheless.

"Who is that white skunk?" asked Quacks.

"Dats my buddy from da big city. Dat's Punk da Skunk!" replied Stranger cheerfully.

"Well, he bought us some time, but I don't think it will last long. We need help and we need it now!"

Not a moment too soon, a great clash of thunder ripped across the sky. Clouds eddied and swirled forming a Fairy door in the sky. In a glow of bright light streaming from the portal that opened in front of them, Oberon, King of the Fairies, Queen Titania, Prince Demone the Gnome, and Sugarplum flew through the opening.

"That's enough!" the King ordered and waved his golden wand over the ghouls, ghosts, and skeletons. A spray of magic fairy dust streamed from its glowing end, coating the massive hoard with sugar. "I order you go back to your eternal rest! Walk these lands no longer. Go back from whence you came!"

The ghosts, wraiths, and banshees howled in anguished, writhed in protest, staggered and contorted in fight but King Oberon's good magic was stronger than the witch's potion and carried the power of Mother Nature behind it.

"Be gone, I say!" the king commanded again.

When the evil hold broke, the wisps raced back instantly to find their individual places of rest. Also impelled by the magic, the hoard of ghouls slowly turned and began their slow trudge back to the graveyard.

The pirates were the last. Being the most evil, they snarled and rattled their swords with arrogance. The raspy voice of Red Beard challenged King Oberon. "You'll have to do better than that to get us back in that swamp, Fairy King!"

The witch's eyes glistened with the hope that all was not lost. "Fight, my beauties. Fight with all your might!" she ordered to the cackled roar of laughter from the pirates.

"Help me, my Queen!" King Oberon called.

Queen Titania flew to his side and together they combined the power emanating from their wands and directed it toward the pirates. Again the pirates writhed and twisted in knots but still they fought off the commanding power.

"Sugarplum, come join us!" the Queen ordered.

Now with the three wands together, the magic was too great and the spell broke. They too reluctantly had to return to their place of eternal rest. As they traipsed back up the hill, the refrain, "Ten men dead on a dead man's chest, Yo, ho, ho and a bottle of rum," faded into the distance.

"This cannot be!" screeched Evilla from afar, still refusing to believe that all might be lost. But she knew she still had her unexpected secret weapon.

Punk had run down from the top of the gazebo and found the warlock's Staff of Change that had fallen from his grip and got snagged in the bushes.

"Stranger! Help me!" he yelled pulling on one end of the shaft.

Seeing Punk's struggle with the oversized stick, Stranger and Pronto ran to help and leapt into the bush, grabbing the other end. With just a couple of tugs they managed to pull the ornate rod free.

Seeing his staff, the warlock swooped down and reached out to grab his weapon of transformation. With the raven still badgering him, and flying low to the ground, he came within inches as the city friends ran. As he was about to snatch the wand, Stranger saw him, yanked hard and veered away pulling Punk off his feet at the other end and swinging him the clinging skunk around in the new direction.

"What the...?" Dreadmore shouted again.

Meanwhile Pronto had jumped up onto the broom, run up through Dreadmore's cloak and used his secret weapon. Rat-tat-tat! The sunflower seeds bounced off his nose in rapid succession distracting the warlock enough to give Punk and Stranger time to get away. The warlock did not know whether to swat the raven pecking at his head or protect his face from the stinging sunflower seeds. In either case, he had failed to get back his Staff of Change.

The flying broom flew erratically; swooping up into the sky then hammer-heading back down. Swerving this way then that, the soaring sweeper spun around buildings, tipped over garbage cans then streaked through a bakery shop's back door and out through a plate glass window. Dreadmore's face and cloak dripped in white frosting from the wedding cake display.

Clearing the icing from his vision, he swerved just in time to avoid the telephone lines as he headed back toward the town square. Finally, when the broom flew close to the band gazebo, Pronto, refilling his cheek pouches, jumped off and slid down the drainpipe to join his buddies.

"That was close," Stranger panted running toward the Gnomes. "Let's get this to the magic people."

"Over here! Bring that staff to me," yelled Prince Demone who could see that Dreadmore had finally gained control of his broom and was heading back for another attack.

The warlock, hugging his broom low, approached fast and was again closing in on Punk, Stranger, and Pronto. He was determined to get his warlock's staff back from these pesky little thieves.

"Give that to meeee!" he screamed.

The trio had scooted from the bushes and now stood out in the open on the short trimmed town square grass. Running as fast as they could while carrying the long stick, they were out of breath and desperate to reach Prince Demone.

Dreadmore smiled an evil grin as he dove in low, thinking he had them now that they were in the open. Just as he was about to grab the staff, the three crafty mammals dodged left and ducked under an old truck parked at the curb.

"Curses!" the warlock yelled but it was too late.

Dreadmore couldn't adjust in time and crunched hard into the passenger door of the pickup. With the warlock dazed, the trio ran out from under he other side of the truck to Prince Demone the Gnome.

"Good boys!" he yelled as they dropped the staff at his feet. Demone snatched the staff, whirled around and fired it at the dazed warlock.

"Zap!"

The electric bolt hit Dreadmore, turning him instantly into a black weasel. Both he and the broomstick fell harmlessly to the ground.

Up in the dark sky the witch, seeing her long time partner changed, screamed again, "Noooooooo!"

Queen Titania grasped and pointed her amulet, as Evilla desperately tried to escape what she knew was about to happen. But it was too late. Titania hit her with the Stone spell bolt from the amulet. With a look on her face frozen in fear, she was instantly changed into a statue of granite and fell from the sky. Evilla and her broom smashed to the ground and shattered.

"All right!" yelled Sneezer.

"Wahoo!" squealed Quacks, doing a jig.

"It ain't over 'til it's over," said Stranger, breaking up the levity.

"What do you mean, 'it ain't over'? The witch is dead, the witch is dead, and the warlock's a weasel!" Quacks sang, locking his arms in

Sneezer's legs and doing a twirl.

Silhouetted by the moon, the wolf like creature stood on a rooftop and howled. "Awooooooooooo!" cried the beast as he pounded his chest and striking fear into living being that heard it.

"What is that!" squealed Quacks.

"I tried to tell ya, Boss" Stranger insisted. "Dat ting rose from a steel coffin in da graveyard pond after da ghouls had left."

"Oh," said Quacks as the smile slid from his face.

"Awoooooooooo!" came the howl again as the beast leapt from one rooftop to another then sprang onto the ground.

"We've seen these blood suckers before!" said the king.

"But it's been a very long time," Titania replied.

"What is that?" Quacks asked.

Queen Titania turned to the heroes. "They come from an evil place. They feed on blood."

"Wait here," King Oberon ordered. "You cannot deal with this without getting hurt." He flew directly toward the beast.

"Your wand cannot change this one, darling," Titania called after the king.

"He has been bitten by evil."

"I must try," shouted the king. He flew on.

"He can't handle that beast all by himself," Quacks protested. "There must be some way we can help!"

"Don't get close to that thing," Titania said with a shiver. "He'll rip you to pieces."

"Okay then, maybe not." Quacks agreed. The little band of heroes froze in their tracks.

"But we can't let King Oberon fight him all by himself," insisted Sugarplum.

"Right, we must help! We have to help!" the group bravely began to march after the king again.

"If he bites you, you will become like him!" Titania cried.

"Whoa!" Quacks flung his arms out halted the group again.

"What's wrong with you scaredy cats? Ain't you just fought snarling pumpkins?" Gerome barked. He'd had enough.

"Yes." Several heads nodded.

"And, ghouls? And zombies and skeletons?"

"Yes."

"And you're gonna let one snarling little doggie scare ya? Are ya?"

"YES!" they cried, quivering. The ferocious wolf's claws grated over the cobblestones as it crept toward the survivors. Its eyes glowed red, and a deep, guttural growl rumbled from its throat.

"Okay, beast!" Gerome shouted, thrusting out his chest. "Don't let fear and common sense stop ya! Have at us."

"Er, I don't think he has any fear," said Quacks, quaking visibly now.

"I don't think he has any sense either, common or otherwise," Sugarplum added.

"Well, he doesn't scare me! Let's go!" Gerome commanded his gnome troops who took off after their king.

Quacks eyed Stranger, Pronto, Punk, and Sneezer. Behind the fear he read there, he saw steely determination. He alone turned and ran after the king and the gnomes.

One by one, the reluctant band of animals followed.

King Oberon waved his wand to cover the beast with fairy dust. It should have frozen the creature but had no affect. "Titania, use your amulet and turn him to stone! Quick!"

Queen Titania flew into position and pointed her amulet up the road toward the heaving werewolf. The amulet glowed and an aura formed around the stone.

Filled with hope they watched as the amulet sizzled into life and the blue aura spiraled through the air.

"Crack!" The stone shattered into thousands of tiny shards of glass as the amulet disintegrated into dust.

"What happened?" the King wailed. The raging beast was now almost upon them.

The king's spell was powered with the essence of good but the beast's enormous strength enabled him to resist its potent grip. He plunged on, eyes glowing red, claws slashing, and jaws gnashing.

"I do not know." Queen Titania gazed down at the pile of dust. "I guess all of its power was drained when we used it on the witch."

"Or maybe this unearthly fiend is too powerful even for our magic!" the king said, struggling to cast another spell. He could feel himself weakening. He needed more time to recovery from the drain of casting the previous spell.

"I don't know if we can hold him much longer!" yelled Gerome, casting an ice storm in the direction of the monster.

"Okay, demon, let's see if you can handle this blizzard!" Prince Demone joined in adding a tornado to Gerome's ice storm. The other gnomes cast giant snowballs and hurl them at the beast.

The werewolf lusted after the warm living blood of any victim he could get his hands on and this unwavering obsession gave him fight strength against the magic thrown at him. King Oberon or his queen would be the tastiest of all.

Duke and the crows came in for one more attack, swooping down, careful of the beast's slashing claws. The crows' diversion gave the gnomes and fairies only a second's rest.

"What else can we use to send this beast back to Hades?" asked King Oberon holding his arms out to cast another spell. "I can't keep this up much longer!"

"Silver," answered Gerome. "We need to strike his heart with silver!"

"Where can we get a silver dagger?" asked Sugarplum.

"Any form of silver will work, if I can get it," Gerome told her.

"Da witches chain," Stranger said, crouching low. "When we freed Sugarplum I saw that the chain holding her keys was made with silver."

"Good idea," said the queen.

"Pronto, Sugarplum, Sneezer, see if you can find the necklace!" Quacks ordered, pointing at the pile of rubble where the witch had fallen.

"We'll need more silver than just a chain," said Gerome. "A lot more. Enough to make a dagger."

The werewolf burst through a giant snow wall, roaring with rage as a barrage of snowballs hit him. Before him another wall had already formed. In fury, he slashed through it, too but while some of the gnomes lambasted him with snowballs, others constructed another wall.

"Duke, come to me," Sugarplum called. He heard her voice and landed on a hydrant next to her. "I recall you had some jewels and coins in your nest," Sugarplum reminded him sweetly. "Can you and your friends get all the shiny white ones for me?"

"Caw, caw, shiny, shiny white," Duke agreed, bobbing his head. The entire flock of crows, plus the raven, set off to the Northwoods roost.

Then Stranger had an idea. Remembering how cold winters in the big city had been, he ran to the fountain and began flinging chunks of granite into it. When Quacks caught on and helped, too. Soon the water in the fountain overflowed onto the street and down toward the struggling werewolf.

"Good idea!" Gerome called, hurling an ice spell over it. The water instantly turned to a sheet of ice and the werewolf's feet slipped out from under him. Because of the pummeling snowballs, even using his long claws, he scrambled to regain his balance.

A speeding blur raced past Stranger toward where Sneezer still hunted through rubble. Pronto had found the necklace but he needed help to carry it. Sneezer glanced up to see Pronto scurry to a pile of broken rocks, and he followed. Flitting along behind him, Sugarplum saw a large piece of round granite shaped like Evilla's head. From beneath it, a set of keys poked out. Pronto leaned into the scrawny-neck-shaped rock but it wouldn't budge. Sneezer pawed at it and pushed it with his nose but it was too heavy even for him.

"Let me see what I can do," Sugarplum said as she sprinkled some fairy dust on the rock. With her tiny arms outstretched and face straining, she attempted to lift the large stone by magic. It wobbled a first but then levitated slowly off the ground. "Hurry," she gasped. "I can't hold this much longer."

Sneezer snatched the set of keys and chain from under the stone just before it crashed back to the cobblestones, shattering.

"Let's go!" she yelled. The chain dangled from Sneezer's mouth as they headed back to the battle.

By the time they had reached the square, Duke and a few of his roost cousins had also returned with several silver coins, a thimble, and a locket. The raven had a silver teapot in his claws.

"Wow! You are a bunch of thieves!" said Quacks.

"Quickly! Get a bucket," ordered Gerome, just returned from the snow front.

Stranger appeared with a washing pail and placed it on the ground. The bits of silver clattered into the bucket.

"King Oberon, Queen Titania, Sugarplum! I need your help here now!" Gerome called. "This will require all the magic we can muster."

Meanwhile, the werewolf smashed through the last wall of ice, nearly slashing several gnomes. Molly and Barley were waiting for him and charged. The werewolf hurtled through the air, splattering on the ground then rolling and tumbling through a fence. His broken neck and arm instantly mended and reformed. Stunned, he shook off the pain, let out a blood-curdling howl and leapt back into the fray.

Angus had finally had enough of this creature and now pawed the ground with his hoof and snorted. "This means war!" he bellowed. The street rumbled with the sound of his hooves. Lowering his great head, he gored the monster with his horns then he pitched his head up flinging beast down an alley and into a dumpster.

Furious, the creature jumped out and straddled the top of the bin. The gore wounds sealed up immediately. With another bellow, charged again.

Gathered around the pail, the fairy king, his queen, Sugarplum, and Gerome joined their power to cast a Melting Spell upon the bits of silver. Instantly the objects started to sizzle, bubble, soften, and dissolve into a molten blob. Gerome rolled the liquid in the bucket as the globule cooled to form a round ball.

"I didn't need a bullet! I need a dagger," said the King, flinging another Frozen Spell at the beast.

"I know. Your Majesty, but I do not have an anvil to forge a dagger," Gerome replied.

"Lets' ram it down his throat," Stranger snarled.

Gerome shook his head. "We can't get close enough without being bit."

"How about ice?" Quacks suggested. "We could use an icicle like an arrow and freeze the bullet inside it."

Gerome formed ice around the silver ball and shaped it into a huge icicle.

"Sneezer, get me a rope," ordered Quacks.

Sneezer loped away and returned draped in clothes and sheets from a nearby washing line that he had pulled down.

"Not quite what I had in mind but it'll do," said Quacks. "Okay, let's stretch this thing out, as tightly as you can."

Stranger ran wrapped one end around a lamp post while Sneezer ran in the other direction and wrapped his end around Angus' horns. Once the line was taut it did not look at all like a bowstring. All of the washing still drooped off the rope. Gerome placed the icicle arrow at the center of the clothesline and, with the help of the others, pulled back.

"Okay, everyone. We got only one shot so let's make it count," said the King.

The other gnomes stopped their snowball and blizzard spells and the werewolf crashed through the last wall. In a rage, he blindly tore forward, flying through the air front claws ready to rip flesh. Then he saw the bolt slicing through the air toward him. His red eyes widened.

"Thwack!"

The giant icicle struck him squarely in the chest. He yelped like a dog and fell to the ground, writhing and whining. His grotesque body finally came to a stop at the feet of the band of heroes.

"Did we get him?" asked Quacks.

"I think so," said Sneezer, sniffing.

"Look!" Queen Titania cried.

"Ooooooh," sighed the rest.

Before their eyes, the beast began to change. Slowly the hair disappeared, the claws retracted, the hands, legs, and face began to look human. All the evil had been replaced with serenity as the man lay on the street.

"Isn't that the old woodcutter?" asked Gerome.

"I do believe you are right," said Sugarplum. "He was such a kindly man."

Then face changed again. The skin slowly turned to fine dust and drifted away on the cool night breeze, followed by his powdery bones. Within moments nothing was left—not one shred of the creature that had moments before terrified the weary band.

"Wow," said Quacks.

"He was some scary dude," Stranger added.

"Don't forget the witch and warlock," Sugarplum reminded them. "They were the ones who started all of this."

"Well they will never bother you or us again," King Oberon declared.

"Thank-you, King Oberon!" shouted Quacks.

"No, I thank-you. All of Fairyland owe you and your band of heroes our utmost gratitude. You will always be in our favour!"

"Oh boy, oh boy! Does that mean we get sweet treats?" asked Sneezer, his ears standing up.

"As many as you wish," the king replied with a smile.

"Carrots and apples?" said Molly and Barley at the same time.

"And shredded wheat covered in sugar?" Angus asked.

"Of course. But our work here is not done," King Oberon said. Curling his finger, he called out the remaining weasels from hiding holes and shadows and from behind crates and boxes. With the witch and warlock gone they didn't know what to do.

Prince Damone picked up the Staff of Change and changed each weasels back into the child each once was. All except one timid black one with a grayish face.

Once changed, the youngsters went running back into the arms of their parents now timidly venturing from their homes and gathering in the town square.

"Is it over?" someone asked.

"Where's my little Jenny?" asked another.

"And my Bobby?"

"Thank goodness you're safe," cried a mother as she gathered her daughter into her arms.

Sugarplum made sure each child had bags filled with sweet treats to make up for their scary night.

Not only were the Weasel Warren children changed, but Sleazel, Meazel, Diesel, and all of the other weasels that had been enslaved by the witch changed into human children, too. With the spell broken, they shook their heads but could not remember anything of their past lives as weasels.

"Where am I?" asked Diesel as he patted himself to make sure he was all together and human.

"I know you," said a woman nearby. "You're the Marshal boy. They've been looking for you for months!"

"And you, you're the Clark's daughter," someone said to Meazel. "We'd better get you home, too. I know someone who is going to be very, very happy to see you!"

Slowly the children rejoined their parents, with the exception of one…Sleazel, a tall, lanky boy holding the black weasel in his arms.

"My name is Simon. Where are we?"

"In Weasel Warren," answered Quacks.

"I heard you. I can understand you." It was as if a thread of memory remained and Simon could understand Quacks.

"Yeah, well don't make a fuss about it," Stranger said. "Where do you live and who are your parents. We'll get you back to them."

"I don't have any parents. They died in a car crash last year leaving me an orphan. The last thing I recall was being unbuckled by an old woman in a black cloak."

"Dat explains it," Stranger blurted.

"What can we do?" asked Sneezer.

"Caw, caw, Farmer McSimmons, Farmer McSimmons, caw," cried Duke from his perch on top of the band gazebo.

"There's a good idea," said Sugarplum. "The McSimmons' never had any children of their own."

"Hmmm, I think you just might have something there, Sugarplum. They are getting older," Quacks said, nodding.

Still unsure if Simon was completely rid of Sleazel, Stranger shared his apprehension with Quacks. "All we need is someone else sticking their nose in around here. Remember, he took a bite outta you. More dan once. And dat thing he's got cuddled in his arms is a special piece of work, too."

Pronto puffed up his cheeks ready to fire.

"Really? I bit him? I don't remember any of that. I wouldn't hurt any of you now," pleaded Simon. "You are my friends!"

"We'll have to see about that," said Quacks. "I do know that we can't just leave you here," he said with a wink to the rest. "Who knows what kind of trouble you might get yourself into!"

Gerome, Sugarplum, King Oberon, Queen Titania, Prince Damone, and the other gnomes said good-bye to their friends and returned to Fairyland through a new portal.

When the aura had disappeared and the quiet of the night returned, "Well, what do we do now?" asked Sneezer.

Quacks smiled and sighed. "We go home."

Bruce Kilby

# Chapter 18

# Back on the Farm

As with all previous mornings, Sneezer woke at the crack of dawn to bark at the crows and the one raven with a chain around his ankle. This day however was a little different than the rest.

When Farmer McSimmons came out of the house he found a young lad sitting on the back porch with Sneezer and petting a black weasel he held in his arms.

"Who are you, boy?" asked the farmer.

"I am Simon, sir, and I followed your dog home last night."

"Followed him home?" Where would Sneezer go at night other than his doghouse, he wondered.

"Yes, sir," Simon said, not wanting to give anything away.

"Have you got no place to go, boy?"

"Not really. I am an orphan."

"Well, I..."

"And I am looking for a place to stay. I got the sense that you might need a little help around here." He smiled toward where Quacks, Stranger, and Pronto hid under a wheelbarrow.

"Well um…Mrs. McSimmons and I never did had any children," he mused. "But I just don't know. What about the authorities?"

"We do need a little help around here." Mrs. McSimmons stood in the doorway of the old farmhouse. "It's not as easy as it used to be. Your back gets stiffer after each harvest, Henry."

Sneezer nuzzled Farmer McSimmons' hand.

"Oh, stop that, ol' fella. Let a man think." He scratched Sneezer's ear. "Well, I guess you could stay on for a bit. We'll have to talk to the Sherriff but in the mean time, there's a lot of work to do."

"Yes, sir."

"So there won't be any slackin' either," McSimmons said with a frown.

"I'm used to hard work, sir."

"And you'll have to go to school!" Mrs. McSimmons added.

"Yes, Ma'am."

"That pet of yours better not get into the chickens or he's a gonner!"

"Yes, sir. I will keep him in a cage and teach him to do tricks," the boy answered.

"Well, okay then, come on in. We'll need to get you cleaned up if you think you're going to stay in this house. Where did you get those clothes? They look familiar. And they're way too small for you. A little brightly coloured, aren't they?"

"They are all I have."

As Simon stepped into the house, he turned and with a grin, winked at Quacks, Stranger, Pronto, Sneezer, and Punk. Duke was feasting on the remains of Sneezer's breakfast and thinking he might take a flight over Rapture Ridge tonight.

Stranger turned to Punk. "I guess you'll be on your way, old friend."

"You know you are more than welcome to stay here if you wanted to," Quacks said. "You've been a great help."

"Thank you, thank you, signore. But I have to get back and look after the family business, if you know what I mean." He brushed a paw under his chin.

"Yeah, yeah, I know," Stranger said sadly. "I miss the old crowd, too. But day can't..."

"No worries Mack, er, I mean Stranger," Punk said, patting Stranger's shoulder. "Your secret is safe with me. Maybe one day I come back to visit."

"You may have to if you get caught by the pound again," Stranger laughed.

"I tink maybe my tagging days are over."

Quacks, Stranger, Sneezer, with Duke riding his back, laughed and giggled as they headed to the pond. Pronto ran off toward the giant sunflowers at the end of the vegetable garden to reload with his favourite snack. You just never knew when more trouble might show up on the farm.

Later that night Farmer McSimmons shouted, "You found my gold pocket watch!"

"I don't think so, honey," Mrs. McSimmons replied, looking up from here knitting. "It has been gone for months. By the way, did you find my broach? Here it is. I can't believe it. I looked in that drawer several times but here it is! And we have some spoons left out on the table that have been missing for a such long time."

"I have no idea where they came from," Farmer McSimmons said. "I certainly didn't find them. Maybe it was the boy?"

"I don't think. You know, that crow has been hanging around here a lot the last little while."

Farmer McSimmons scratched his head. "By the way, the darnedest thing happened today. I can't figure it out. How did all those pumpkins get back into the field?"

"I have no idea, sweetheart but today has been a very good day," said Mrs. McSimmons. "A very good day indeed!"

Free Chapter Plates may be downloaded for colouring, and CDs are available for purchase, from www.firesidestoriespublishing.com.

Made in the USA
Columbia, SC
23 July 2021